Enid Blyton's
LITTLE ANIMAL STORIES

Enid Blyton's
LITTLE ANIMAL STORIES

PURNELL
London

SBN 361 01807 X

Published in 1971 by Purnell, London, W.1.
Text © 1971 by Darrell Waters Ltd.
Artwork © 1971 by B.P.C. Publishing Ltd., London, W.1.
Made and printed in Great Britain by Purnell & Sons Ltd.
Paulton (Somerset) and London.

CONTENTS

Wagger Goes to the Show

"Mummy, there's to be a garden-party at the Hall, in the grounds, next month!" said Terry, coming in with his sister Alice and his dog Wagger. "Can we go?"

"There's to be all kinds of fun," said Alice. "There's a donkey to give rides, and all sorts of competitions, and swings and ice-creams. We *can* go, can't we, Mummy?"

"Yes, of course," said mummy. "You must start saving up your money at once, then you will have a nice lot to spend."

"And, Mummy, there's a baby-show," said Alice. "Isn't it a pity we haven't got a baby, because then it might win a prize at the baby-show. I expect Mrs. Brown's baby will win. It's the fattest baby I ever saw."

"Oh, it isn't always the fattest babies that are the best ones," said mummy. "Well, I'm afraid you can't take a baby. You're my baby, Alice, and you're seven!"

"Let's put Alice in for the baby-show," said Terry with a grin.

"I'm not a baby," she said. "Oh, there's a dog-show too. We're going to put Wagger in for that. What sort of a dog is he, Mummy? There are classes for fox-terriers, and spaniels, and pekes. What is Wagger?"

"Wagger isn't any special kind of dog, I'm afraid," said mummy. "He's what we call a mongrel—just a mix-up of a dog. He's not pure-bred like the fox-terrier next door. He's a very ordinary, rather ugly mongrel."

"Mummy!" said both children in horror. "He's *not* ugly! He's beautiful."

"Well, darlings, you think he's beautiful because he's yours and you love him," said mummy. "But he isn't really beautiful. His tail is too long. He's too big. His ears aren't quite right. He'd never win a prize at a dog-show." Wagger looked up at the children and wagged his long plumy tail. They stared down at him, looking into his bright eyes.

"I didn't know he was a mongrel," said Alice. "I didn't know he was a mix-up dog. I thought he was the nicest dog I ever knew. I still think so."

"So do I," said Terry and he gave Wagger a stroke on his head. "And I'm going to take him to the garden-party even if all the dogs there turn up their noses at him! He'd hate to be left behind."

"Well, don't put him into the dog-show," said mummy. "Everyone would laugh at him, he's such a peculiar-looking dog. Yes, I know he's a darling, and faithful and loving—but he *is* ugly!"

The children went out, with Wagger jumping beside them. They simply couldn't see that he was ugly at all. "He's got the nicest eyes!" said Terry.

"And the loveliest ways," said Alice. "Does it matter so much that he's a mongrel? Oh dear—it's a shame he can't go in for the show."

"Well, he mayn't be the most beautiful dog, but he's the happiest and healthiest," said Terry. "We look after him much better than they look after their dog next door."

"Yes, we do," said Alice. "Wagger always has good meals and fresh water every day. And we bath him properly, and brush his coat well every morning. And he has good warm straw in his kennel in the winter, and lots and lots of walks all the year round."

"Wuff," said Wagger, licking Alice's hand.

"He understands every word we say," said Alice, and she hugged him. He licked her face all over.

"Don't be upset because Mummy said you were ugly," said Alice. "*We* think you're lovely, Wagger."

"Wuff," said Wagger happily. He wagged his long tail so fast that it could hardly be seen.

The children saved up their money that month. They ran errands and weeded the garden, and cleaned Daddy's bicycle, and whatever they were paid they put into their moneyboxes. Soon they had quite a lot of money.

"It's the garden-party tomorrow," said Alice to Terry one day. "Mummy's washed my blue frock for me. And you've got new shorts to wear."

"We ought to make Wagger look nice too," said Terry. "Let's give him a bath with plenty of soap and warm water. And we'll brush his coat till it shines."

"I wish we could clean his teeth too," said Alice.

"His teeth always do look white and clean," said Terry. "He wouldn't like you to do that. I wish we had a new collar for him. His is old and rather dirty-looking."

"Well, that won't matter," said mummy. "He's not going in for the dog-show, so he doesn't need to be all dressed up in new collars and ribbons. So long as he is clean and healthy, that's all that matters when you take him out with you. Get out the little tin bath if you want to wash him."

They bathed Wagger between them. He was as good as gold. He never made a fuss about being washed like the dog next door did. He just stood in the warm water and let himself be soaped all over. He even shut his eyes so that the soap wouldn't get into them. He was as clever as that!

The children rinsed him and dried him. Then they took turns at brushing his thick, silky coat. It was rather curly, and it was fun to see the curls come up under the brush.

They even brushed his big ears and his long tail. He looked very fine indeed when they had finished with him. He capered about in delight, barking.

"I still think he's beautiful," said Alice, looking at him. "He's such a happy-looking dog. His eyes are so bright, and his tail is so waggy. Wagger, you're a darling!" Wagger licked her and pranced off again. He was certainly a very lively dog, always ready for a walk or a game.

Next day the children set off to the garden-party,

with Wagger at their heels, freshly brushed. They paid their sixpences at the gate and ran to have a ride on the little grey donkey. Wagger ran beside the donkey all the way round the garden and back.

Then they had ice-creams, and Wagger licked up all the bits that dropped on the ground. After that they went to have a swing, and Wagger waited on the ground below, because he didn't like swinging.

Then they all went to see the babies at the show, and Alice was glad she wasn't the judge, because she thought all the babies were as nice as one another. Terry didn't like them so much. He said they made too much noise, and their faces were ugly when they screwed them up to cry.

Then they had another ice-cream each, and spent some money trying to fish prizes out of a pretend fish-pond with a little fishing rod. But they weren't lucky, and couldn't hook a single prize! Wagger watched solemnly, and once he wuffed as if to say "I'm sure *I* could hook a prize if I had a chance!"

Then a bell rang, and someone called out that the dog-show was about to begin. Everyone with dogs hurried to the big tent. What fine dogs there were, to be sure. Terriers dancing about on neat little legs. Pekes, with their snub noses, looking rather haughtily around. Scotties and Sealyhams barking loudly with excitement. Really, it was all very thrilling!

"We'll go in and see the show," said Terry. "But we'd better leave Wagger outside, as we can't show him. It's a shame! Poor Wagger. He can't help being a mongrel."

They tied Wagger up outside the tent and went in. There was a ring of sawdust inside, and here people walked their dogs round and round when they were showing them. The children watched, and the judges, sitting nearby, made notes and talked in low voices to each other.

Then they called out which dogs won the first prize and second prize. The fox-terrier who belonged to the family next door won second prize and got a red ticket. His owner, a big boy called Ray, was delighted.

"See, Terry," he said, as he passed him. "I've got second prize for Nobby. Pity your dog's such an awful mongrel!"

Then one of the judges got up to speak. "We have now awarded all the prizes for the various breeds of dog," he said. "But there is one special prize to come, for which any dog can be entered, whatever breed he is. This is a prize given for the best-kept and healthiest dog. Please bring your entries to the ring one by one."

So one by one the dogs were all brought up. Ray brought his Nobby too, proudly wearing the red ticket marked "Second" in his collar.

And then a dog walked into the ring all by himself! The children gasped. It was Wagger! Somehow he must have wriggled himself free and come to find Alice and Terry. He walked into the ring of sawdust, looking all round for them.

The judges thought he was entered for the competition. One put his hand on Wagger's collar and looked at his teeth. Wagger didn't mind at all. He just

20

wagged his tail hard.

The judges ran their hands over his coat. They looked at Wagger's eyes. They lifted up his feet and felt down his legs. Wagger barked joyfully. He thought they were making a nice fuss of him.

Wagger was the last dog in the ring. One of the judges looked round the tent and called out loudly: "Who owns this dog? Will he please come forward?"

Rather scared, Alice and Terry went into the ring. Wagger greeted them with loud barks, licks and jumps.

"We—we didn't mean . . ." began Alice. But the judge interrupted her.

"Ah, so you own this lovely dog," he said. "Well, I am pleased to say that we shall award him the prize for being the healthiest and best-kept dog in the show.

21

His coat, his teeth, his spirits are all first-class—a very
fine specimen of a dog, and most intelligent."

And, to the children's enormous surprise, one judge
handed Terry a white ticket marked "FIRST" in
big letters, and another judge handed him a new
collar for Wagger, and a big box of chocolates for
themselves!

"Oh, thank you," said the children, and Terry said,
"But—he's only a mongrel, you know."

"Any dog can enter for this kind of competition,"
said the judge, smiling. "It's for the best-kept, healthiest dog—no matter what kind he is, pure-bred or
mongrel. You deserve the prize for keeping your dog
in such good condition."

Wagger barked and licked the judge's hand. The

children turned away in delight, and bumped into Ray, who was holding Nobby on a lead.

"We've got a First," said Terry, beaming. "Oh, Ray—Wagger's got a First, and Nobby's only got a Second. I've never had such a surprise in my life."

"Let's go home now," said Alice. "I want to tell Mummy. Let's go quickly. And we'll give Mummy the box of chocolates, because it was she who taught us to keep Wagger so well and happy."

So they left the garden-party and tore home to tell Mummy the good news. She was just as surprised and delighted as they were. She hugged them all, Wagger too.

"We must all share the chocolates," she said. "Wagger, you look fine in your new collar. Really, you look beautiful!"

"He does, he does!" said Terry. "And he's going to have his share of the chocolates, just for once. Three cheers for old Wagger, the best dog in the show!"

"Wuff, wuff, wuff!" said Wagger, three times, and made everyone laugh. Really, he's a very clever dog indeed!

Paying It Back

THERE was once a dog called Mack. He was a little dog with a big bark, and every one was very fond of him. He lived with Terence and Hilda, and they took him for a walk each day.

They were good to Mack. They always saw that he had plenty of good food to eat, and filled his bowl full of fresh water each day. They brushed him well every morning, and made quite sure that he had plenty of straw in his kennel at night.

Terence and Hilda had two pets. One was Mack and the other was a big goldfish called Rudolf. Rudolf had lived in the nursery ever since the children could remember. He had a very big round glass bowl, with some pond-weed in it, and he swam round and round the bowl and looked at the children through the glass.

He knew Mack the dog very well indeed, for he had seen Mack brought into the nursery when he was a tiny puppy, so small he could hardly walk. The goldfish had looked and looked at the puppy. He had never seen one before, and he wondered what it was.

When Mack grew older he wanted to see the gold-fish properly. The glass bowl was always put in the middle of the nursery table so that the children could see the big red fish swimming whilst they were having their meals. He looked lovely peeping at them between the pond-weed in the bowl. When the children fed him he popped his red nose out of the water and ate the food greedily. He would take some from the children's hands, so you see he was really very tame.

One day Mack jumped up on the nursery table to have a good look at Rudolf the fish. He lay down on the table with his nose close to the bowl and watched the goldfish. Then he wuffed to it.

"Why don't you come out and play with me?"

"Because I should die if I left the water for long," said the goldfish, poking his nose out of the top of the bowl to speak to Mack.

"It must be dull swimming round and round in your bowl," said Mack.

"I have plenty to look at," said Rudolf. "I love to see the two children, and it's fun to see you come trotting into the nursery too. You are a very nice dog."

Mack was pleased. He wagged his tail so hard that it thumped the table like a drum.

"Oh, I say! What's that funny noise?" said the goldfish in alarm.

"Only my tail wagging," said Mack. "It's to say I'm friendly to you. Wag your tail at me, goldfish, and then I shall see that you are friends with me too."

"I can't wag my tail like you," said Rudolf. "If I wag my tail it makes me swim fast and I shall bump

27

my nose on the bowl. But I'll waggle my fins—look!"

Rudolf waggled his fins and Mack thumped his tail again. Then he heard someone coming and he jumped off the table. He was not really supposed to climb up there.

After that Rudolf and Mack were very friendly indeed. Rudolf always got excited when Mack came into the room and Mack always gave a little bark to tell Rudolf that he was pleased to see him. Once Mack even jumped up on the table and dropped a few biscuit crumbs into the water for the goldfish. Rudolf was delighted.

Now one very, very hot day somebody upset Mack's bowl of water. It always stood outside in a shady spot. Perhaps the gardener trod on it and upset it. Maybe the window-cleaner upset it. Mack didn't know. Anyway, the water was spilt and Mack had none at all.

There was no pond in the garden. There was not even a puddle to drink from, for the weather had been hot and all the puddles had gone.

So Mack had nothing to drink at all. He went about with his tongue hanging out, feeling so hot that he wished he could take his coat off as Terence did.

The children were out for the day, so they did not see that Mack was thirsty. Their mother was busy, and the maid never bothered about Mack anyhow. So nobody knew that the little dog was dreadfully thirsty. He went to his overturned bowl and tried to lick a few drops out of it—but there were none. So off he went again, his pink tongue hanging out, dry and thirsty. The sun shone down hotly, and made him more thirsty than ever.

The evening came. The children arrived home, laughing and talking. They noticed Mack's tongue hanging out and called to him, "Go and have a drink, silly dog!"

"Wuff!" said Mack. But they didn't understand that he was saying that his bowl was empty. They went off to bed and left Mack downstairs. Night came and the poor little dog really thought he would die of thirst. He went up to the nursery and lay down panting on the floor.

Rudolf the goldfish spoke to him. "What's the matter, Mack? You look hot."

"I am so thirsty I think I shall die!" said Mack. "My bowl of water has been spilt and nobody has given me any more."

"You poor thing!" said Rudolf. "Well, come up here on my table, Mack—and have a drink out of the water in my bowl!"

"Oh, tails and whiskers, what a good idea!" wuffed Mack. "Do you really mean it?"

"Of course," said Rudolf. "You are my friend, aren't you? And friends should always help one another. But leave me enough water to swim in, won't you? If you drink it all, I should die."

"I'll leave plenty," said Mack, and he jumped up on to the table. He put his tongue into the bowl of water and lapped it up greedily. Oh, how delicious it was! Mack had never ever tasted such delicious water.

"Leave me enough to swim in!" cried Rudolf, as

the level of the water went down and down. "Stop! Stop!"

Mack stopped drinking. He could have drunk the whole of the water, he was so thirsty. He had left just enough in the bottom for Rudolf to lie in—it was very little indeed.

"Bones and biscuits, I hope I've left enough!" said Mack in dismay. "Will the children fill your bowl to-morrow, Rudolf?"

"Sure to," said Rudolf, waggling his fins to and fro. "Don't worry about me. I'm all right so long as I keep still. There's just enough to cover me."

"It's very, very kind of you," said Mack gratefully. "I can't tell you how much better I feel already. I will do *you* a good turn one day, Rudolf. I really will. I will pay back the good turn you have done me, I promise you."

Rudolf laughed and made a few bubbles in the water. "You won't be able to pay it back," he gurgled. "Dogs can't help goldfish!"

But Rudolf was wrong, as you will see. Not very long after that, there came an enormous thunderstorm. It was right overhead, in the very middle of the night. The thunder sounded like wardrobes falling down the stairs—crash-crash, rumble, smash-crash! The lightning flashed and the whole world was drenched with rain. The children woke up with a jump, but they liked thunderstorms, so they didn't mind a bit. They lay and waited for the lightning to light up their bedroom.

Mack growled at the storm. He was angry with it

32

for waking him. He was lying in his basket in the kitchen, and he heard the raindrops come pelting down the chimney nearby.

Rudolf the goldfish was dreadfully frightened. "This must be the end of the world!" he thought, and he swam round the bowl like mad. The lightning came into the nursery and Rudolf jumped in fright. Then such a crash of thunder came that the fish leapt right out of the water! He fell on the table and wriggled there, gasping.

He couldn't get back into the bowl. He flopped about in alarm, wondering what was going to happen to him. He could only breathe when he was under the water. He would die!

He wriggled right off the table—plop! He fell on to the floor and flapped about there, jumping and gasping for all he was worth.

"Help! Help!" panted poor Rudolf. "Water! Water!"

The children did not hear him—but Mack did! Mack pricked up his ears when he heard the plop. Then he was puzzled to hear some wriggling noises on the floor overhead, and he at once ran up the stairs to see what they were.

And on the carpet lay poor Rudolf, gasping for breath! "Oh, Mack, I shall die if I don't get back into my bowl!" he panted. "The thunder frightened me and I jumped out."

Mack looked at the poor goldfish. He did not dare to take him into his mouth and try to put him back, for he knew his teeth would hurt him. But whatever was he to do? He couldn't leave his friend like that.

So Mack lifted up his head and began to bark. How he barked! Wuff, wuff, wuff! WUFF, WUFF, WUFF! He went on and on, and at last every one in the house heard him and came running to see what the matter was.

And there they found Mack sitting close beside the poor goldfish, barking for all he was worth! Terence at once lifted Rudolf up and slipped him gently into his bowl of water. How thankful the big fish was! He breathed again and swam round his bowl in delight.

"Fancy! Rudolf must have jumped out with fright!" said Hilda. "What a good thing Mack knew! Aren't they kind to one another! First Rudolf lets Mack drink his water—and then Mack rescues Rudolf!"

They all went back to bed—but Mack stayed in the nursery.

"I've paid back your kindness," he said to Rudolf, with his paws on the table. "I've paid it back, just as I said I would. It's a nice feeling!"

"Thank you," said the goldfish, waggling his fins. "You're a real friend, Mack. You saved my life."

It *is* nice to pay back a bit of kindness, isn't it? I always try to if I can, don't you?

Boom-Diddy-Boom-Boom!

JACK and Katie went down the garden looking very sad. They came to their duck-pond at the bottom and looked at the ducks swimming there.

"You're losing all your dear little ducklings," Katie said to them. "The fox comes at night and takes them. You be careful of yourselves, too, ducks, because the fox may take *you* next!"

"It's a pity old Rover doesn't hear the fox about," said Jack. "He doesn't wake till the ducks quack loudly in fright—and by that time the fox is away with the ducklings!"

"Let's play down here this morning," said Katie, setting her dolls down on the grass. "Then if the fox is hiding anywhere near, maybe we'll scare him."

Jack put down his toys, too. He had brought his drum, his boat to sail on the pond, and his kite. But there wasn't enough wind for the kite, so he sailed his boat.

They played there all day. One of the dolls was tied in the boat and went for a sail. Her feet got rather wet, but she liked the sail very much. She told the other toys about it when she got back.

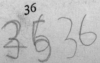

"The boat bobbed up and down," she said. "The little waves rippled all round—see how they splashed my feet!"

Katie noticed that the doll's feet were wet and she sat her in a sunny spot to dry. When it was time to go in she collected all her toys and so did Jack. But Katie forgot to fetch the doll with wet feet and went indoors without her.

The doll was upset. She looked round for the other toys, but they were all gone except the drum, which Jack had left near the pond and had forgotten. The doll got up and went over to it.

"I'm lonely," she said to the drum. "I'll sit by you. I hope Katie comes and fetches us soon. I'm frightened of the fox that comes each night and steals the little ducklings. He might steal *me*."

Rover the dog was in his kennel some way off. "I'll look after you," he called.

"You're not much good!" said the doll. "You never wake up till the fox has gone and the ducks are quacking for help!"

"He's so soft-footed," said Rover. "Ah, he's a cunning fellow, he is!"

He lay down and fell asleep. The doll could hear his little snores. The ducks put their heads under their wings and slept too. The little ducklings cuddled together in a crowd and shut their bright black eyes.

The doll stayed awake beside the drum because she was frightened in case the fox might come and catch her. She watched all the shadows around, wishing that Katie hadn't forgotten all about her.

And then she saw two bright eyes looking out of a bush! She heard the soft breathing of the fox. She knew he was there, waiting to pounce on the little ducklings again—and perhaps to pounce on her, too. What could she do?

If only Rover would wake up! But he was fast asleep. The doll tried to call out but her voice wouldn't come, she was so frightened. And then she caught sight of the drum in the moonlight.

She groped for the sticks that belonged to it. She found them and stood up bravely. She hammered on the drum with the two little wooden sticks.

"Boom-diddy-boom-boom, boom-diddy-boom-boom, boom-diddy-boom-boom," went the drum loudly in the night, and Rover woke up with a jump. He was out of his kennel in a trice. He smelt fox at once! The fox crouched back in his bush, scared by the sudden, startling noise of the drum.

"Woof, woof, boom-diddy-boom-boom, woof WOOF!" went Rover and the drum together, and the fox raced out of the bush in terror. After him went Rover.

And Rover caught him! He pounced on the fox who stole and ate ducklings, and dragged him back to the garden. Out ran the children's father with a stick, and out ran the children too, in their night-clothes.

"Rover's got the fox!" cried Katie. "Now our little ducklings will be safe. Oh, Jack, listen—what's that noise?"

It was the drum, of course, which the doll was still

beating desperately. Boom-diddy-boom-boom, boom-diddy-boom-boom!

The doll stopped when she saw everyone running to Rover. She was trembling, but how glad she was that she had saved those dear little ducklings. All the ducks were awake now and quacking loudly in fright.

Katie suddenly saw her doll sitting by the drum.

She ran and picked her up. "Oh, you poor little thing, did I leave you out all alone? And look, Jack, here's your drum! I say—*was* it the drum that was making that noise we heard?"

"Couldn't have been. Who could have beaten it?" said Jack, picking it up.

"My doll did," said Katie. "And that woke up

43

Rover—and he chased the fox at once, before he could get the ducklings. Daddy, Daddy—it was my doll that beat Jack's drum and woke up Rover in time to catch the fox!"

"Rubbish!" said Daddy. "Get off to bed now, both of you. We shan't be worried by the fox again, that's certain!"

But even though Daddy said it was rubbish, Katie hugged her doll, and as a reward for her cleverness she let her cuddle into bed beside her. Jack let the drum stand beside his pillow all night long. It couldn't help feeling proud.

And you should have heard the doll telling all the other toys about her adventure the next day! They could hardly believe their ears!

Brer Rabbit's Strange Flower

ONCE upon a time Brer Rabbit took his garden spade and dug out a little round bed right in the very middle of his garden. He edged the bed with shells and watered the ground thoroughly.

"What are you doing, Brer Rabbit?" asked Brer Fox, leaning over the fence.

"Oh, good morning, Brer Fox," said Brer Rabbit, very busy indeed. "I'm just getting this bed ready for the marvellous Minny-Pinny Flower."

"The *what*?" said Brer Fox, in astonishment. "I've never heard of it."

"Ah, I don't wonder," said Brer Rabbit. "It's a most strange flower, Brer Fox. It has purple petals, a red centre, yellow leaves with blue spots, and a most exciting smell. But the strange thing about it is that only those people who are truthful and honest can see it or smell it! Dishonest people can't see or smell the Minny-Pinny Flower at all!"

"My!" said Brer Fox, grinning. "Then what's the use of *you* growing it, Brer Rabbit? You won't be able to see it when you want to plant it! Ho! ho! ho!"

He went off and left Brer Rabbit scowling. Soon the news about the marvellous Minny-Pinny Flower had spread and every day people came to see if it was there. One day Brer Hare saw Brer Rabbit digging a hole in the middle of the bed, and he watched to see what he was going to plant. Brer Rabbit pretended to pick up something and was very busy seeming to plant it in the hole. Then he patted down the earth, took his watering can and watered it thoroughly, and looked up at Brer Hare.

"Hey-ho, Brer Hare!" he said, grinning. "You're just in time to see me plant the strange Minny-Pinny Flower. Isn't it queer? Come in and smell it."

Now Brer Hare had heard that only truthful and honest people could see the Minny-Pinny Flower— and he couldn't see anything in the bed at all. He was filled with horror. If he said he could see nothing Brer Rabbit would at once say, "Oho, Brer Hare, you're dishonest, then—only dishonest people can't see my marvellous flower!" And then Brer Hare would feel perfectly dreadful! What ever was he to do?

"Do come in," said Brer Rabbit, opening his gate. "Can't you smell the Minny-Pinny Flower from here? It's a most exciting scent."

Brer Hare went in. He thought he had better pretend to see the flower and admire it. It would never do if people knew he couldn't see it. They would say he was dishonest at once. So he went up to the bed and bent over as if he were smelling the flower.

"Marvellous!" said Brer Hare. "Oh, what a fine flower! How strange it is! How beautiful!"

47

Just then Brer Terrapin poked his nose in at the gate and saw Brer Hare admiring the flower that he, Brer Terrapin, couldn't see at all! "My!" thought Brer Terrapin. "If Brer Hare can see it, it must be there! I'd better pretend I can see *something*!"

So in he waddled and was soon pretending to smell the marvellous Minny-Pinny Flower, too. Brer Rabbit leaned on his spade and looked pleased. "It's a strange flower, isn't it?" said Brer Rabbit. "And the smell— ah, stranger still! Look at the queer leaves, yellow with blue spots! Truly a wonderful plant! Now, my friends, I shall soon know who is honest and who is dishonest in our town, for, as you know, dishonest people can neither see nor smell this plant!"

Brer Hare and Brer Terrapin went home, and on their way they told everyone about the strange Minny-Pinny Flower, and how they had seen it and smelt it— though, of course, they had seen nothing at all! Soon all the folk were hurrying to Brer Rabbit's to see the strange plant, and Brer Rabbit grinned and waved his hands as they leaned over the fence.

"Hey-ho, Brer Bear! Hey-ho, Brer Wolf! Hey-ho, Brer Turkey Buzzard! What do you think of my lovely Minny-Pinny Flower? Come in and smell it. If you want seeds from it, I can sell you a packet at two-pence a time!"

Now, of course, Brer Bear, Brer Wolf and Brer Turkey Buzzard could see nothing at all in the bed, but not one of them liked to say so. It would never do to let the others know such a thing—it would be dreadful to be thought dishonest or untruthful!

"Wonderful!" said Brer Bear.

"Marvellous!" said Brer Wolf.

"Such a fine scent!" said Brer Turkey Buzzard.

"It's a useful plant to have in your garden," said Brer Rabbit. "It soon shows you who tells the truth or not. Would anyone like any seeds?"

"I'll take a packet," said Brer Bear, and Brer Wolf and Brer Turkey Buzzard said the same, so Brer Rabbit gave them each small envelopes—but when

49

the three opened them to look at the seeds they could see nothing at all! Dear, dear, how dreadful not to be able to see even the seeds! They felt most ashamed, and hid it by exclaiming that the seeds were marvellous too! Then off they went home, talking about the Minny-Pinny Flower and their wonderful seeds, but all of them secretly very much worried because they could see nothing at all.

The next day everyone came to look over the fence again, hoping that they would be able to see the flower that morning. Brer Frog hopped up too, and goggled his big eyes at the bed—but Brer Frog was an outspoken person who never pretended anything at all. So he opened his wide mouth and croaked: "Well, where's this marvellous flower? I can't see anything at all! There's nothing there—and you know it, Brer Rabbit! It's just one of your tricks!"

Everyone stared at Brer Rabbit—but he didn't turn a hair. No, not he! He leaned on his spade and spoke very sadly. "Brer Frog," he said, "you're quite right. My Minny-Pinny Flower died in the night, and I've dug it up. So there *is* nothing in the bed at all. But it told me who were truthful and who weren't!"

Then everyone grew very red, for they knew Brer Rabbit had tricked them. One by one they stole away —all except Brer Frog, and he croaked at the grinning rabbit: "You're a fraud, Brer Rabbit! Nothing but a fraud!"

"I'm no worse than anyone else," said Brer Rabbit, grinning. "Am I now?" And Brer Frog had nothing to say to that!

Benjy, Benjy, Benjy!

THERE was once a little black spaniel puppy who was still with his mother. He hadn't yet gone to his new home.

But he was going that very day! His mother licked him all over carefully and gave him some good advice. "Don't make friends with strangers. They may want to steal you away. Always sleep with one ear open at night in case thieves come to rob your master's home. Never bite anyone unless you are certain that it is your duty. And be sure to come when you are called."

"Why?" said Benjy. "It's a nuisance to have a name, and to have to hear it and go running off when I'm in the middle of something exciting. I don't want to have a name."

"Don't be silly," said his mother. "All dogs have names. Yours will be Benjy. I heard the children who are going to have you say that your name will be Benjy. It's a very nice name."

"Well, I shan't come when I'm called," said the puppy. "Even if I hear my name I shan't come."

"I shall bite your ear if you say that again," said his mother sharply. "All dogs must come when they are called. I do, and I'm old now."

Benjy didn't say any more in case his mother bit his ear. But he had quite made up his mind he wouldn't answer to his name. What, stop sniffing down a rabbit-hole just because somebody wanted him? Stop playing with another dog just because he was called? No, not he! He would be the Dog Without a Name. That was a very, very good idea.

So, when he went to his new home, he pretended not to know his name at all. James called, "Benjy, Benjy, Benjy!" dozens of times, but Benjy didn't so much as turn his head. Pam called, "BENJY" as loudly as she could, but he really might have been deaf for all the notice he took.

"He can't be as stupid as all that," said their mother, vexed. "I believe he's just naughty."

"Oh, Mother—he's sweet. Don't smack him because he won't come when he's called," said Pam.

"Well, if he doesn't learn soon, he'll have to be smacked for being disobedient," said Mother. "A disobedient dog is as bad as a disobedient child—you can never depend on them or trust them. Benjy—come here!"

Benjy was playing with a ball, having a lovely time, when Mother called him. He heard his name, of course, and pricked up his ears—but he didn't run to Mother as he should. He just went on playing with his ball.

"There!" said Mother. "He heard me call and he knew his name—but he didn't come. He's naughty. He must really be smacked."

"Oh, dear," said Pam. "He's so little. I do hate him to be smacked. Mother, give him a chance for a day or two."

"Very well. I will give him three days to learn his name and come when he's called," said Mother. "He isn't stupid. He's just naughty and obstinate. He always enjoys what he is doing too much to leave it and run to us when we call him. Three days, Pam and James—and no more!"

Mother went out of the room. The children looked at one another.

"Isn't Benjy tiresome?" said James. "He really does hear his name and he knows it, Pam; I see him prick up his ears, or even look round when we call him, but he won't come!"

"We'll have to make some kind of a plan," said Pam. "Or else he'll always be getting into trouble. After all, if Mother won't stand any nonsense from *us*, she certainly won't stand any from Benjy. You might be certain of that."

So they thought hard. Pam took her big teddy bear on her knee to nurse, whilst she thought about their difficulty.

She looked down at her teddy. "I know *he'd* come all right if only he could, if I called him," she said. "He's a darling."

They both looked at the big, fat old teddy bear and he looked back at them out of his glassy eyes. Then James gave a chuckle.

"I know! I've thought of something funny—and I believe it will work. Let's pretend that *Teddy* is called Benjy, instead of the puppy. And whenever we have anything nice for Benjy—his dinner, or a biscuit, or a bit of an ice-cream, or a ball to play

54

with—we'll call 'Benjy, Benjy', as usual, and then we'll pretend that *Teddy* is Benjy and give him the treat!"

"Oh yes—you can call him and I'll walk him over to you, like we do when we pretend he's alive," said Pam. "That's an *awfully* good idea!"

"Let's begin this very minute and see how our plan works," said James. "You take Teddy over there and sit him by you. I'll go and get a sweet biscuit, the kind Benjy loves. I'll call 'Benjy, Benjy,' and he won't take any notice, as usual. Then you must walk the teddy over to me, and I'll say, 'Good Benjy, good little Benjy, here's a biscuit for you!' "

"And you can pretend to give it to him, and I'll take it quickly and put it into my pocket, so that Benjy will think the teddy has eaten it," giggled Pam.

James went off to get a biscuit. Pam took the teddy to a chair and sat him beside her. The puppy was playing with a rubber ball in the other half of the room, rolling over and over on his back, enjoying himself.

James appeared again, with a biscuit. "Benjy, Benjy, Benjy!" he called. Benjy took not a bit of notice. He knew James had a biscuit for him, but he wasn't going to leave his game and fetch it. Let James bring it over to him as he usually did!

But what was this? The teddy bear was lifted down, and, guided by Pam, was walked clumsily over to James! "Good Benjy, good little Benjy!" said James, in a very pleased voice.

"Isn't he *clever*?" said Pam, loudly, and she patted the bear. "Eat your biscuit, Benjy bear!"

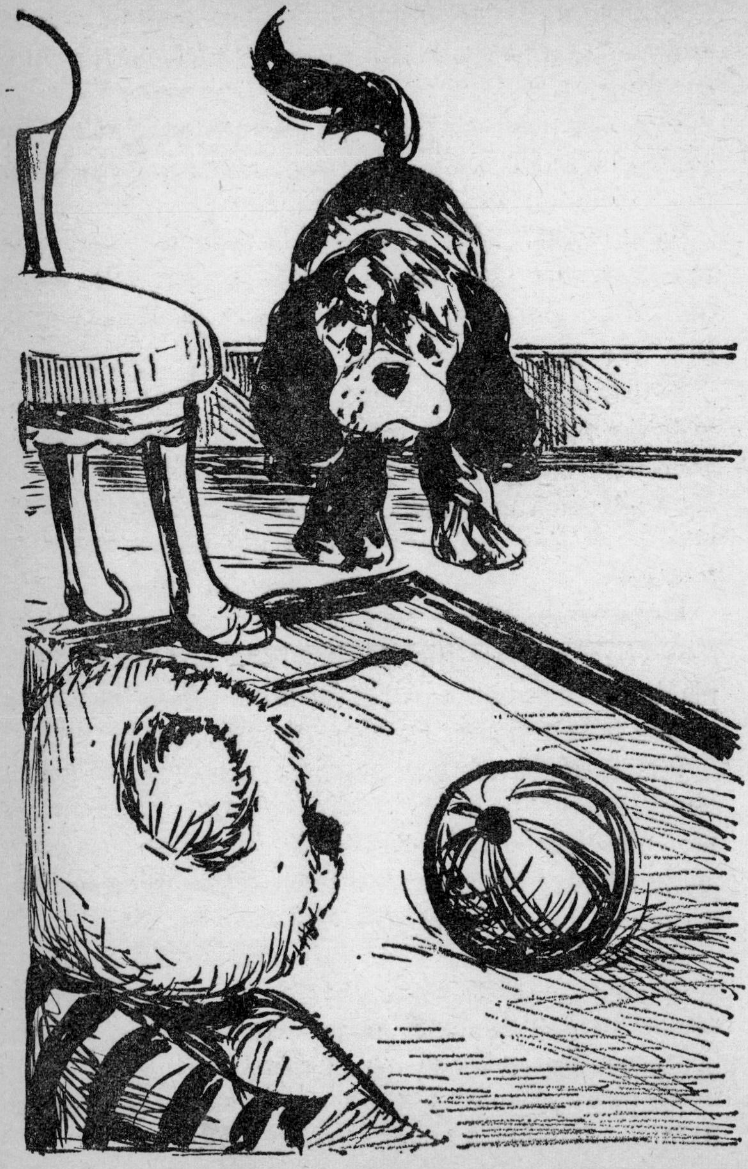

She slipped the biscuit into her pocket just as Benjy the puppy came running over, upset and puzzled. Why were they calling the bear "Benjy" and giving him biscuits? He was only a silly toy. Benjy sniffed at him. Gracious, he must have eaten that biscuit! It was gone!

James and Pam laughed. "The trick is working already," said James. "We'll do the same thing with his ball in a minute. Go and get it now, Pam, whilst he's sniffing round the bear."

So Pam went and picked up the ball when Benjy wasn't looking. James sat down by the bear. Benjy wandered off in disgust. That bear! Answering to *his* name and eating *his* biscuit! Didn't the children know that the bear wasn't Benjy? It was really very puzzling.

He looked for his ball. It had disappeared. Pam had it, of course. She called loudly: "Benjy, Benjy, Benjy!"

The puppy heard, but took no notice. He saw that no biscuit was about, so he went on looking for his ball. But, good gracious me—that bear was walking over to Pam, his arms gently held by James!

"Good little Benjy bear," said Pam, patting him. "Clever little Benjy bear. Here's a ball for you to play with."

And to the puppy's dismay his pet ball was rolled on the floor for the bear to play with!

"Grrrr!" said Benjy, and dashed at his ball. That bear wasn't going to have it. He couldn't *imagine* why the children laughed so much all of a sudden.

They made such a fuss of the bear. "Poor little Benjy bear—did he lose his ball? Nasty little puppy to take it away from him!"

Benjy made up his mind that he would bury his ball deep down in the garden, and he ran off. The children looked at one another and laughed.

"Perhaps in three days he will have learnt to come to us when his name is called!" said Pam. "It rather looks as if he will!"

Well, the next time they called Benjy was to get him for his dinner. Usually they called and called and rattled the dish, but Benjy took no notice, although he knew it was his dinner time. Why call him? Let them put it down and he'd go to it—but not because he was called.

"Benjy, Benjy, Benjy!" called James—and once more Pam walked the big teddy bear quickly over the floor to where James stood with a dish of dinner. And to Benjy's horror the bear put his nose into the dish and appeared to be eating his biscuits and meat! Of course, it was really only Pam putting his nose down for him, but Benjy didn't know that. He was horrified. He rushed over, barking and growling.

He gobbled up his dinner very, very quickly in case the bear ate it first. The children patted and stroked the bear, but they didn't pat Benjy at all.

"Poor little Benjy bear! Did the puppy eat up the bear's dinner, then?" said Pam, and cuddled him lovingly. Benjy felt very left out. He wanted to be patted, too—but this horrid bear seemed to get all the love that was going.

"Your name is *not* Benjy. You are not to answer to it. It's *my* name, do you hear?"

"Well, why don't you answer to it then and go when you are called?" said the kitchen cat, washing herself as thoroughly as she always did.

"Grrrrr!" said the puppy, and then backed away as the cat spat at him.

For three days the children made a fuss of the bear, walked it about whenever they called "Benjy, Benjy, Benjy," and gave it all kinds of treats. Benjy got very tired of it, indeed. On the third day Mother came into the playroom and looked for Benjy.

"Has he learnt his name yet? His time is up now. Benjy, Benjy, Benjy!"

Pam waggled the bear's legs—but Benjy the puppy was first! He shot over to Mother at once and looked up at her. She gave him a bone she was carrying. "Well!" she said. "It really does look as if he's learnt his name at last. James, go down into the garden and call him. If he comes to you, I shall be very pleased. Pam, stay here, and when he has gone down to the garden, call him up here and see if he comes."

James went off. "Benjy, Benjy, Benjy!" he called. And off shot Benjy down the stairs, slithering down the last four and out into the garden.

Then Pam called him in her turn. "Benjy, Benjy, Benjy!" And into the house and up the stairs he sped at top speed, right up to Pam.

"Well, I'm quite satisfied," said Mother, pleased. "I shan't smack him, because there won't be any need to."

And from that time Benjy knew his name and answered to it, always coming when he was called, no matter what he was doing. Everybody thought what an obedient little fellow he was. But he won't make friends with the old teddy. He just simply won't! He growls whenever he sees him, and I'm not a bit surprised, are you?

The Cat Who Cut Her Claws

THERE was once a most beautiful cat called Smoky. She was the colour of blue-grey smoke, and had long thick fur and lovely golden eyes. Everybody thought she was wonderful.

Smoky thought herself wonderful too. When she sat washing herself on the wall, she loved to see people looking up at her, and saying, "Oh! Look at that marvellous cat!"

The other cats thought she was lovely too, but they didn't tell her so, because they thought that she was vain enough already.

"You know," said Cinders, the black cat, "Smoky is really rather stupid. She can't even catch a mouse!"

Now Smoky was just the other side of the wall, and she heard what Cinders said. She jumped up on to the wall and spat at Cinders in a very rude way.

"I am very clever indeed!" she said. "*You* may not think so—but the two-legged people do. They are always telling me so! Why, I can even rattle at a door-handle to tell people I want to get into a room."

"Really!" said Tabby, a grey-striped little cat. "Well, I don't do that, Smoky—*I* just jump in at the window!"

61

The cats laughed, and Smoky jumped down in a temper. She went into her house and looked for her mistress, who always made a great fuss of her. She was in her bedroom, dressing herself ready to go out.

"Hallo, Smoky darling!" she said. "What a beauty you are! But what have you been doing to your lovely fur? You have dust on it!"

Smoky's mistress took a little brush that she kept specially for the cat and brushed her fur well. Smoky purred. Ah, what did other cats know about having their fur brushed? What other cat had a basket with a silk cushion in it? What other cat had a white china bowl with her name on, as Smoky had?

Smoky sat and looked at her mistress. She saw her wash her hands and face. "I do that too," thought Smoky, "but my tongue and paws are my soap and sponge!"

Then her mistress brushed her hair. "My hair has been brushed too," thought Smoky proudly. "I am really much more like a two-legged creature than a cat!"

Her mistress sprayed herself with a sweet-smelling scent. Smoky sniffed the smell and liked it. She stood up and mewed to her mistress.

"What! You want some scent too!" said her mistress, laughing. "Very well! I will spray you with some!"

So Smoky had some scent like her mistress, and she felt so proud that she really couldn't sit still any longer but went prowling up and down the room, purring loudly.

"And now I must do my nails!" said Smoky's

mistress, getting out her little nail-scissors and file and
tiny bottle of varnish.

"Ah! Nails!" thought Smoky, and came close to
see what her mistress was going to do. "Mistress
always calls her claws nails. What does she do to
them? I must watch."

Smoky watched her mistress trimming her nails

and filing them shorter. She watched her paint them with a little pale-pink stuff from the tiny bottle, to make them shiny.

"There!" said Smoky's mistress, showing the cat her nails. "Don't they look nice? They are not horribly sharp and long like *yours*, Smoky! Oh, how I should hate to have cats' claws! Good gracious! Look at the time! I must run or I shall miss my bus."

She ran downstairs and left Smoky in the bedroom. Smoky looked at the nail-scissors and file and tiny bottle. So her nails were horribly sharp and long? Well, why shouldn't she cut them and paint them a pretty pale pink so that they shone like glass?

"I'm washed, I'm brushed, I've got scent on me," thought Smoky. "And now I don't see why I shouldn't make my claws into nails. I shall *really* be like my mistress then!"

So what do you think that vain cat did? She cut off the sharp points of her twenty claws. She filed them down neatly. Then she tried to put the shiny varnish on them out of the little bottle. But she upset the bottle and made a great mess on the carpet!

She put out her claws and dipped them all into the spilt varnish. Then she let them dry, and soon they were as shiny as her mistress's had been. How proud Smoky was!

"I must go and show all the other cats," she said. "They will certainly think I am clever to have nails instead of claws!"

So off she went, and miaowed so loudly that every cat from the gardens around came running at once.

Smoky sat on the ground and looked at the cats with her big golden eyes.

"Look how clever I am!" she said, putting out her short, blunt, shiny claws. "I have nails instead of claws. I watched how my mistress did it—and now I am like her. Smell me, too—she put some of her scent on me!"

The cats looked at the strange claws in surprise. They turned up their noses at the sweet smell that came from Smoky.

"You are foolish," said Cinders. "Very, very foolish. You think you are clever—but you will soon find out how silly you are, and you will be sorry that you have nails instead of claws."

"You only say that because you are jealous of me," said Smoky grandly. "I know that you all wish you had nails instead of claws—but I shan't tell you how to get them. That is my secret!"

"We don't want to know," said Tabby.

"Hark! A dog!" cried Cinders suddenly. He was right. In at the gate rushed a big dog, his pink tongue hanging out, his eyes gleaming to see so many cats to chase! "Wuff!" he said, and rushed at the little crowd of frightened animals.

Tabby rushed up a tree. Cinders leapt up the fence. The others ran for their lives, and so did Smoky.

Smoky had such a curious and unusual smell that the dog chose to chase *her*! So down the garden went Smoky, and after her went the dog, barking madly.

Smoky was terrified! She ran and ran and the dog ran too. "I must jump up a tree!" panted poor Smoky.

So she ran to a tree, and tried to claw her way up it.
But alas for Smoky, her claws were now only short
blunt nails and she could not dig them into the bark
of the tree and hold on as she leapt up. She fell down
to the ground again and the dog nearly caught her!
Off she went again, feeling more afraid than ever.
She couldn't even fight the dog, for she had no claws
to claw him with! Oh, how could she have been so
foolish as to make her fine claws into useless nails!

Goodness knows what would have happened to poor Smoky if Cinders and Tabby hadn't come to her rescue. They knew that she now had no sharp claws and would sooner or later be caught by the dog, so up they ran. One leapt on to the dog's tail and one clawed at his hind legs. The dog turned to snap at the two cats, and that just gave Smoky the chance to jump right over the wall and run home.

She hid behind the sofa, panting and puffing. She felt very silly and very much ashamed.

"I've been so vain and foolish that I nearly got caught by a dog!" she said to herself. "I shall let my claws grow very, very long! Oh, how I hate the look of them now—silly, useless nails!"

That evening Smoky told Cinders and Tabby how sorry she was for being so silly, and she thanked them for saving her. "If it hadn't been for your good strong claws I would be chewed up by that horrid dog by now!" she said. "Forgive me for being vain and foolish. I see now that I am not at all clever. Please teach me to catch mice when my claws have grown."

"Very well," said Cinders. "Maybe your mistress will like you better still if you have claws to catch mice with, instead of nails to make you vain!"

Cinders was right. Smoky's mistress was delighted when she began to catch mice. "I thought you were a silly, beautiful cat without any brains at all!" she said, hugging Smoky. "But now I see that you are as clever as you are beautiful!"

The Five Bad Boys

"WHERE are you going, you two?" asked Mother, as Donald and Jeanie went out of the door.

"Just to take some of the carrots we've grown to that dear little donkey in Farmer Straws' field," said Jeanie. "Look, Mother—aren't they fine carrots?"

"They are," said Mother, "and you're fine gardeners. All right, take the little donkey a feast. He's certainly a dear little thing."

"Mother, would he be very expensive to buy?" asked Donald. "You know how Jeanie and I have always wanted a pony of our own—and as we can't have that we wondered if a donkey would cost a lot of money."

"Yes, I'm afraid it would," said Mother. "And anyway we couldn't keep it in our tiny garden. You must just be content with going to see other people's horses and donkeys."

The two children went off with their carrots. The baby donkey was certainly adorable. He came running to the field gate as soon as he saw them, because he knew them very well.

"Hello, Long-Ears," said Donald, rubbing the grey velvety nose. "How are you this morning? Very hungry?"

The donkey's mother stood nearby, proud of her youngster. She never tried to come and eat his carrots. The children liked her too—she was so round and gentle and soft-eyed. She had often given the children rides.

A stone suddenly flicked against the little donkey's nose and it started back in alarm. "What's up, Long-Ears?" said Donald, surprised. Then another stone came flicking over the hedge and hit the donkey on the back. He ran off to his mother.

Donald and Jeanie looked round. "It's those boys again," said Donald, in disgust. "The Gang—Harry, John, Ronnie, Peter and Sam. They think themselves so grand and fine, going round making themselves a nuisance, ringing bells and running away, throwing stones and stealing fruit."

A squealing noise came to Jeanie's sharp ears. "What's that?" she said. "That squealing? It sounds like some animal that's frightened."

They listened. Now Donald could hear it, too. He went out of the field and looked down the lane. The gang of boys were standing together, looking at something in the middle of the group.

"They've got a pup, I think," said Donald. "What are they going to do with it? They are such cruel boys that you never know what they'll do if they get an animal into their power."

Jeanie went pale. "Oh, Donald—don't say they've

got a little pup and they're going to ill-treat it!"
she cried. "You know how they stoned that poor
duck the other day. They're horrible boys."

The boys *had* got a little pup. They were jabbing it
with sticks, and it was squealing. But when a car
came by they hurriedly picked up the puppy and
stuffed it into a sack so that it could not be seen.

"Did you see that?" said Jeanie. "They've put it
into the sack. What are they going to do with it,
Donald? Poor, poor little thing."

The gang of boys set off down the lane. Harry had
the sack over his shoulder. John jabbed at it with his
stick and grinned when a squeal came out of the
sack.

The boys forced their way through a gap in the
hedge and went over to a pond in the field beyond.
Jeanie and Donald stood in the gap and watched them.

Ronnie undid the sack and out tumbled the poor
little puppy. It crouched down on the ground, terrified
and bewildered. Then Sam took it by the scruff of the
neck and threw it right into the middle of the pond.

"Let's see how you swim!" he shouted, and all the
boys laughed. Splash! The puppy landed in the water
and began to try and swim at once, its short little
legs beating to and fro.

"Oh, Donald! Let's go and save it!" said Jeanie,
tears in her eyes. But Donald held her back. He knew
the boys would turn on them and knock them down,
and he didn't want Jeanie to be hurt.

"Now they're throwing stones at it to stop it getting
out of the water," said Jeanie, beginning to sob.

71

"Let me go, Donald. I don't care what they do to me. I'm going to help the puppy."

The puppy squealed in terror when the stones hit it as it struggled to get to the edge of the pond. Once it reached the edge, but John picked it up and threw it back into the middle again. It was getting weak now, and could hardly swim at all.

"It'll drown, it'll drown," wept Jeanie. "Oh, you are a coward, Donald, not to save it."

72

But Donald knew that far from saving the puppy he, too, would be thrown into the pond. He must save the puppy in another way. He was watching for two of his friends to come along. They were to meet him—then they would soon save that puppy!

"There they are!" he said suddenly, seeing Jim and George down the lane. "And Will's with them, too." He beckoned urgently, and the three boys came at a run.

"What's up?" said Will.

"That Gang again," said Donald. "They've got a pup, and they're stoning it in the pond. It's hurt and half-drowned, poor thing. Come on—let's go for those boys and get the pup."

The four boys, followed by Jeanie, ran into the field, yelling. The Gang looked round. Like all bullies, they were cowards, and when they saw how fierce and angry Donald and the others looked they were afraid.

"Come on, run!" shouted Ronnie, and the whole Gang took to their heels and fled. The puppy was left squealing and floundering in the pond. Donald ran to the edge of the water. He and Will waded in and picked up the trembling little creature. It was bleeding from the stones, and was dripping wet and half dead with fright.

Donald tucked it into the warmth of his coat. Jeanie stroked its wet little head. The other three boys looked on in silence. They all loved animals and felt a fierce anger when they saw the tormented little puppy.

"It's such a dear little thing," said Jeanie, tears still running down her cheeks. "I think it must be one of Farmer Straws'. I know his collie had a lovely litter, and this little pup must have wandered away and been found by the boys."

A loud voice hailed them from the gap in the hedge. They looked round. Farmer Straws was there, looking very angry. "What are you doing in this field? Haven't I told you kids time and again not to trespass? Well, this time I'll take your names, and report you to the police."

"Sir, we went in to rescue this little pup," said Donald, showing the farmer the puppy cuddled in his coat. "Some boys were stoning it in the pond. Is it one of your collie pups, sir?"

"Yes—one was stolen yesterday," said the farmer. "Who's been stoning this poor little thing? And who's been stoning that young donkey, too? I saw stones flying over the hedge yesterday and hitting him, but when I went to see who it was, there was no one there."

"Same boys as stoned the pup, sir," said Jim. "We're going after them now. We'll bring them to you sir, and you can deal with them."

"Good lads," said the farmer. "Stick up for the weak and those that can't help themselves, and you won't go far wrong. It's lads like you that can stop other boys from doing these things. Go and get those boys and bring them to me."

Jeanie went to the farmhouse with Mr. Straws, to let the farmer's wife see to the puppy. On the way they passed the field where the little donkey was, and when he saw Jeanie he came running to the gate.

"I do love him," said Jeanie. "I suppose he isn't for sale, is he, Mr. Straws? Donald and I would save up every penny if we could buy him."

"No. He's not for sale," said the farmer. "I'm giving him to my nephew as a present next week."

"He's very lucky, then," said Jeanie, and gave the little donkey one last pat.

Meanwhile, Donald, Jim, George and Will were hunting for the Gang. "Better capture them one by one and take them to Mr. Straws," said Donald. "We'd never hold them all at once. We'll get Harry first."

They got both Harry and Sam. The two were very frightened and tried to get away, but the four boys held them firmly, and took them off to Mr. Straws, who promptly locked them into a shed, till the other three of the Gang were found. Before long Donald, George, Will and Jim had got all five.

Mr. Straws unlocked the shed, and ordered the five trembling boys to stand up in front of him. Outside, to their horror, they saw the village policeman, tall and stern, with a big black notebook in his hand.

"Constable, these boys trespassed on my land this morning," said Mr. Straws. "They also stole a valuable collie pup of mine. They threw it into my pond and stoned it. I want you to take all five to the police station."

"No, no, no!" cried Ronnie, in terror. "My mum would cry her eyes out."

"Let us go!" begged Sam. "My dad would give me such a whipping if he knew we were taken to the police station."

"So would mine," said Harry. Peter and John were so frightened that they couldn't say a word.

"By rights I should throw you all into the middle of my pond and then throw stones at you," said the farmer. "You mean, cowardly, wretched little bullies! You wait till the news gets round, and see what people say about you! Constable, take them away."

"Don't take us to the police station—all the village kids will see us, and we'll never hear the last of it!" said Sam. "Sir, I'll never do such a thing again."

"What you all want is a sound, hard whipping," said Mr. Straws. "Just so that you will know what

pain feels like. You hurt that puppy—you hurt my ducks the other day—you stoned my donkey. You deserve to be well hurt yourselves, so that you may know what pain is. Constable, do you think these boys' fathers would whip them well, if I send them home instead of having them taken to the police station?"

The constable looked at the trembling boys. "I'll have a word with each father," he said, shutting his notebook. "We'll let the fathers choose. Either I take the boys to the police station and charge them, or their fathers whip them all—in front of you, sir, so that you know they're getting what they deserve."

"Right," said Mr. Straws. "Find out straight away, Constable."

Well, you can guess what happened. Not one of the fathers wanted the policeman to take their boys to the police station, and, my word, what a whipping each one got. They squealed as loudly as the poor little puppy had squealed when the stones hit it.

"It serves them right," said Donald to Jeanie that night. "They'll never throw stones again!"

He was right. They didn't. They were frightened and ashamed, and the Gang broke up at once. But that isn't quite the end of the story.

Farmer Straws sent to Jeanie and Donald and asked them to come and see him. They went, wondering what he wanted.

"It's about that little donkey," said Farmer Straws. "I'm not giving him to my nephew now. You see, he was one of those boys who stoned the pup—John Lewis. I'm not handing out any animals to him. I

want the donkey to go to someone kind and decent—
and so I'm giving him to you and Jeanie."

"Oh, *sir*!" said Donald, and Jeanie laughed aloud in
joy.

"And mind you give your three friends a ride!"
said Farmer Straws, with a twinkle. "The ones who
helped to catch those five bad boys."

"We'll go and tell George, Will and Jim this very
minute!" said Jeanie. "But there are five boys who
will NEVER have a ride on Long-Ears the donkey!"
I know who *they* are, and so do you!

Big-Foot Is Very Clever

THE BROWNIE Big-Foot came knocking at the door of his friends' cave late one night. Little-Foot opened the door and peeped out.

"It's me, Big-Foot," said the brownie. "I've a most important letter here to be taken to old Mother Twinkle away on Breezy Hill."

"Oh dear—and I've such a bad leg," said Little-Foot. "I can't walk all that way. You'll have to take it yourself, Big-Foot."

"I can't. I've got to go back tomorrow morning early," said Big-Foot. "Get Swift-One the red fox to take it. He knows Breezy Hill very well."

Big-Foot stayed the night. In the morning what a surprise! The ground was covered with dazzling white snow!

"Look at that! I'll never be able to get to the fox's den through all the snow, with my bad leg," said Little-Foot.

"Never mind. Maybe he has passed by here this morning," said Big-Foot. "I thought I heard him bark not long ago."

"Well, we don't know which way he went!" said Little-Foot.

"*I* can tell you!" said Big-Foot. "I can read foot-prints in the snow even if *you* can't!"

"How can you?" said Little-Foot, surprised.

"Well, just look here," said Big-Foot, pointing to some tracks in the snow. "I know that Hoppity the sparrow walked there—see his rows of little three-toed footprints set together in pairs—and, look, Web-Toe the duck walked there—you can see the mark of her webbed feet."

"So you can," said Little-Foot. "And what are *these* bird-prints? They're not in pairs like Hoppity's."

"Oh, they probably belong to Freckles the thrush or Glossy the blackbird!" said Big-Foot. "They are set one behind the other, see—not in pairs like the sparrow's."

"This looks like a horse's big print," said Little-Foot, getting interested. "And this is a cow's, because the hoof-print is split in half, like the cow's foot."

"Yes—and here's a cat's neat print," said Big-Foot, "and here's a dog's."

"Surely you can't tell the difference!" said Little-Foot.

"I can. The cat draws her claws in when she walks, but the dog doesn't—so you can see the mark of his *claws* as well as the mark of his *paws*," said Big-Foot. "And—oh good—here's the print of the red fox!"

"It's just like a dog's! You can't tell it is the fox's prints!" said Little-Foot disbelievingly.

"Oh, can't I!" said Big-Foot. "Well, Swift-One has a bushy tail, hasn't he—and look, here and there are marks in the snow where it brushed against it! Those are the fox's prints, and if you follow them, Little-Foot, you'll soon find him, and you can give him the note for Mother Twinkle. Goodbye!"

Little-Foot set out after the fox, and followed his prints in the snow. He soon found him and gave him the note. Then he followed his own footprints back home!

Big-Foot was clever, wasn't he? See if you can be as clever when the snow is on the ground!

Boo! Boo! Boo!

Harry was to go and stay with his aunt and uncle at Tall-Trees Farm. His mother took him there, and Uncle Jim and Aunt Nell looked at the small, quiet boy.

"Harry's so shy," said his mother. "He's timid, too —jumps at the least noise. I do hope you will see that the dogs don't jump up at him, because if they do he'll be terribly frightened."

"It would be easier to train Harry not to be timid than to teach dogs not to come jumping around us," said Uncle Jim. "A farm's no place to come if you're going to scream whenever a dog comes near!"

"Oh dear! I do hope you will be gentle with Harry," said his mother. "He really is so shy. Good-bye, Harry. Enjoy yourself, and do what you are told."

Harry was scared of coming to the farm. He was afraid of cows and sheep, he thought the horses were far too big, and he couldn't bear the dogs that came bounding around. Uncle Jim hadn't much patience with him, but Aunt Nell was sorry for the little boy and tried not to let him be frightened.

But, really, Harry was too silly for words! When a hen came clucking round his feet, he screamed for his aunt. "Aunt Nell! Aunt Nell! This hen's going to attack me! She's pecked at me!"

Aunt Nell came running at once—but when she saw that it was only a hen Harry was frightened of, she laughed. "Oh, Harry! How can you be so silly? Look, the hen has seen your shoe-lace is undone, and it looks like a worm to her. That's what she's pecking at."

Now, one day Harry left the gate of his aunt's garden open, and when the geese in the field beyond wandered near it, one of them walked right in at the gate.

It saw the nice green rows of lettuces in Aunt Nell's garden, and went to peck at them. Peck, peck, peck! Those lettuces soon disappeared.

Harry was just by the gate when the goose came in. It was a big bird with a very long neck, and Harry was terrified to see it come walking in at the gate. He saw it go to his aunt's lettuces and eat them. He

84

crouched under a bush, hoping that the goose would not see him. He was so afraid of it that he hardly dared to breathe.

Soon his uncle came by, and saw the goose. In a rage he ran at it, and soon that goose was flying for its life to the other end of the field. Then Uncle Jim saw Harry, hiding under the bush. He was most astonished.

"What are you doing there? Didn't you see that goose eating your aunt's lettuces? Why didn't you chase it away?"

Harry crawled out from under the bush. "Oh, Uncle—it frightened me. It looked so big and fierce. I wouldn't have dared to chase it."

His uncle looked very angry. "Now, see here!" he said, with a frown. "I never thought I'd meet a boy who couldn't say boo to a goose. Never! I'm ashamed of you. Something has got to be done about this. Hiding from a goose, indeed! Not even daring to say boo. Little coward. You're not shy, you're cowardly, Harry."

Harry began to cry, so you can see what a silly he was. "Now stop that," said his uncle. "I'm not your mother or your aunt, ready to rush to you with a handkerchief—I'm your uncle, and I'm going to teach you a lesson."

"Oh, no, no," wept Harry, thinking his uncle was going to whip him.

"Oh, yes, yes," said Uncle Jim. "Now you'll see what I'm going to do. You're to stand here—just by the gate—come along."

Harry went and stood by the gate. Uncle Jim opened it. "Now I'm going to chase a goose into the garden," he said, "and you are to get it out. Understand?"

"But it won't go out for me," wept Harry.

"You say boo to it, and try," said Uncle Jim. "How old are you—eight years, or eight months? Good gracious me, what a baby you are! Now, just you stand there and say boo!"

So, very frightened, Harry stood by the gate and watched his uncle chase a goose towards him. It came flapping in at the gate. Harry was so terrified that he could hardly open his mouth. But at last he did.

"Boo!" he said. It was rather a feeble boo, but at least it *was* a boo.

The goose stared at him, frightened, but it didn't go away. "Boo!" said Harry again, seeing his uncle coming along.

The goose gave a frightened cackle and shot out of the gate at once. Harry was most surprised, and very relieved. He stopped crying.

"Here comes another!" cried his uncle, and sent in a second goose, which was hissing fiercely.

"Boo," said Harry, and the goose shot out of the gate just as the other had done.

"Now this one!" called his uncle. "Oh, there are two coming!"

And two enormous cackling geese came in at the gate, and seemed as if they were going to walk straight over to Harry.

"BOO!" he yelled, half-frightened. And the geese fled away on their big feet as fast as they could.

Harry was astonished and very pleased indeed. Gracious! The geese were really much more scared of him than he was of them!

"Now these hens!" called his uncle, and Harry saw a little flock of hens coming along, attracted by the noise. They walked in at the gate, clucking at each other. They knew quite well they shouldn't go into the garden.

"Shoo!" said Harry, and the hens shooed away at once.

"Aha!" said Uncle Jim, coming up. "So you can say boo to a goose and shoo to a hen. You're growing up! See that I don't have to teach you lessons like this again, or I shall be so ashamed of you that I shall send you home."

Harry thought about the geese and the hens that night. "Fancy my being scared of them when they are

87

so scared of *me*," he thought. "No wonder Uncle Jim thought I was such a coward. All the same, I am a coward really. I can say boo to a goose and shoo to a hen now, but I don't think I could say: 'Come to heel, sir!' to Uncle Jim's big dog!"

Still, he tried it the next day, when Rover was jumping about round him, splashing him with water from the puddles in the farmyard. Although he was frightened of the big dog, Harry spoke to him sternly, in the kind of voice he had heard his uncle use.

"Come to heel, sir! How dare you! Come to heel!"

And Rover put down his tail, and came quietly over to Harry, standing with his nose almost touching the little boy's ankle.

"It's marvellous," said Harry, patting Rover to make him put up his tail again. "I feel quite different!"

Now, two days later, somebody left the garden gate open again, and this time seven cows wandered in! They went straight to the rows of peas that Aunt Nell had grown and began to munch them, pods and all.

Harry saw them from the window, and screamed: "Aunt Nell! Quick, the cows are in the garden!"

But Aunt Nell was out, and Uncle Jim was over in the big barn, a good distance away. Only Harry was there. He watched a cow with long, sharp-looking horns pull down half a row of peas, and begin to munch happily. The little boy knew how proud his aunt was of her peas, and he was upset. But how could he deal with cows? They were not geese or hens that could be booed or shooed, or dogs to be told to come to heel. They were big, heavy, lumbering creatures, with horns that could hurt if they were stuck into anyone.

"I'm scared," said Harry, beginning to tremble. "I really am frightened of cows. I daren't go out into the garden. Yes, I'm a coward all right, even though I thought I wasn't any more."

The cows started on some beans. Oh dear—those were for next Sunday's dinner! Harry suddenly forgot that he was a coward and ran out.

"Boo!" he yelled. The cows lifted their heads and stared at him, but they didn't take more notice than that. They went on munching and munching.

"Shoo!" yelled Harry, but they didn't take any notice of that either.

"Well, come to heel then, you bad creatures!" shouted Harry, wondering if they would, and hoping that they wouldn't. They didn't, of course. They just went on munching.

"What am I to do?" thought Harry. Then he saw the nearest cow looking at him, and he thought she was staring at him very scornfully, thinking, "Ha! What a little coward!"

"I'm not, then!" shouted Harry, and he darted indoors to the hall. He found his uncle's walking-stick and ran out again. He brandished it at the cows.

"Bad cows! Get out! Go away! See this stick, it's for cows who won't go when they're told!"

The cows didn't like the look of the stick. The one nearest to Harry lumbered away to the gate. Harry yelled again, and actually ran at a big red-and-white

cow. She put down her head and he stopped, not liking the look of her horns. She mooed and Harry almost jumped out of his skin. He turned to run away, but managed to stop himself.

"Go away, I tell you!" he shouted, and waved his stick again.

And then, to his great relief and delight, the big cows all turned and lumbered out of the gate!

When the last one had gone, Harry shut the gate. He was shaking at the knees, but he was very pleased with himself. Then he heard a voice from behind him, and he jumped.

"Well, well, well! So he's not a coward after all! He can chase out big cows with horns, as well as boo at geese and shoo hens away!"

It was Uncle Jim. Harry turned and gave a rather trembly smile.

"They went out all right, didn't they? But all the same, I was scared, Uncle. I'm still a coward at heart."

"If you can be brave when you are feeling scared, that's better still," said Uncle Jim. "That's the stuff that heroes are made of, Harry. I shan't call you a coward any more. You're not!"

Harry was very happy at the farm after that. He wasn't scared of anything at all, not even of the big bull who bellowed at him.

It was a good thing his uncle taught him to say boo to a goose, wasn't it?

Adventure in the Woods

ONE beautiful moonlight night Johnny couldn't sleep. He sat up in bed and saw the moonlight streaming over his bed. Shadow, his lovely sheep-dog was lying at the foot, on an old rug.

When Johnny sat up, Shadow awoke. He lifted his big head, cocked his ears, and looked at his master.

"Shadow! I can't sleep!" said Johnny. "It's too beautiful a night to waste. Let's go for a walk on the hills, shall we? Just you and I together?"

"Woof!" said Shadow, in a low voice, for he knew they must not wake Johnny's father and mother. The boy slid out of bed and dressed quickly. Then he and Shadow crept out of the room, and were soon in the farmyard.

The moonlight shone down, and everything could be clearly seen. The ducks were on the pond, quacking, and Jessie, the farmyard dog, lay outside her kennel, awake.

"Where are you going?" she asked Shadow, in surprise.

"Out for a walk with Johnny!" said Shadow,

joyously, wagging his plumy tail. "I've never done this before—gone out in the moonlight. I've often wondered why people don't do it—the world is lovely and pale and quiet then. We're going out on the hills."

They were soon there. The sheep lay dotted on the hillside, half-asleep. Rafe and Tinker greeted Shadow as he and Johnny passed them.

"Hallo! You're out late, aren't you!"

"Off for a walk with Johnny," said Shadow, proudly. "Where are Bob and Dandy, the other dogs?"

"Bob's over there, outside the shepherd's hut," said Tinker. "I don't know where Dandy is. He went off early this morning and hasn't come back. You know what he is for wandering away. Still, we're pretty busy with the sheep just now—I'm surprised he hasn't turned up."

The big sheep-dog wagged his tail at Shadow and then lay down quietly again. Johnny patted Tinker and Rafe and went up the hill, Shadow close beside him.

Shadow wondered where Dandy had got to. It was strange that he hadn't returned before night. He ran beside Johnny, sniffing at all the smells they passed, enjoying the moonlight walk.

Then suddenly he heard a faint and faraway sound. It was so distant that at first Shadow didn't think he had heard anything. Then it came again. The big sheep-dog stood still, his ears cocked well up.

"Come on, old boy," said Johnny. "What are you standing there like that for? There's no one about tonight. Come on—I want to get over the hill."

Shadow trotted on again. Then, on the wind there came that faint sound once more. Shadow stood still and listened, puzzled.

"Shadow! Whatever's the matter with you!" shouted back Johnny impatiently. "I shan't take you out at night again if you don't keep with me."

Shadow ran to his little master once more, but his ears were listening all the time. And when the wind blew around him again, bringing with it that faint sound, Shadow knew what it was.

It was the far-away whine of a dog in pain. And that dog must be Dandy!

Shadow looked at Johnny. The boy was running down the other side of the hill. The moon was so bright that Shadow could even see the pattern on his stockings. Johnny was all right. He knew his way back. Shadow felt that he really must go and see what had happened to Dandy.

He stood and barked loudly to Johnny, hoping that the boy would understand. Then he turned and ran quickly down the hill again, into the valley, and made for the woods that lay on the next hill to the east.

Johnny was puzzled when Shadow disappeared. He called and whistled, but Shadow was out of hearing. The boy went back a little way to see if the sheep-dog was rabbiting, but there was no sign of him.

"It's too bad of Shadow," thought Johnny, vexed. "He always keeps with me when he is out for a walk. Why should he leave me? I won't take him out again!"

He went on by himself, wondering where Shadow was. The sheep-dog was far away by that time, running tirelessly on his strong legs. He came to the wood, and then the wailing sound he had heard came again, much louder because it was nearer.

"It *is* Dandy!" thought Shadow. "Poor old Dandy. What can have happened?"

He ran swiftly towards the sound and came to where Dandy was lying in the wood. Shadow ran up to him and barked. "What's up? Why don't you come home?"

Dandy answered with a pitiful whine. Then Shadow saw that the poor dog had his foot caught in a steel trap. It had been set for rabbits, and was a cruel thing with steel teeth that bit into an animal's leg and held it fast. Dandy hadn't seen it and had put his foot right into it. Now he was held tight and was in great pain. The trap was too heavy for him to move or he might have dragged it along with him.

Shadow tore at it with his teeth, but Dandy stopped him. "That's no use," he said. "I know these traps. I can only get my foot out if someone opens the trap, and only people know how to do that. You can't open it."

"I'll go and fetch someone who can," said Shadow, and he looked anxiously at Dandy, who had lain his head down wearily on his good paw. The dog was tired out with pain.

Shadow ran off, his heart beating fast because he ran so swiftly. He must get help for Dandy. He must not let him suffer one minute's more pain than he could help. How his poor foot must hurt him! How wicked those steel traps were!

Shadow ran back to the farm. Johnny had got back now and was in his bedroom, about to take off his coat. Shadow padded into the room and went up to him. But Johnny pushed him away.

"Shadow, I don't want you! You left me to-night. The moon might have gone in and left me in the dark, and I might have got lost. I am ashamed of you. Go away."

Shadow's heart sank when he heard Johnny talk to him like that. He licked his hand, but the boy took it away. Then Shadow took hold of his sleeve and gave it a gentle tug. That meant, "Please come with me!"

"If you think I'm going to take you out for a walk again, you're wrong," said Johnny, crossly. "And I don't want you to sleep on my bed to-night. If you're going to run off and leave me when I want you, I don't want you to sleep with me."

Shadow felt as if his heart was breaking. Johnny had never said such a thing to him before. The dog pressed himself close to the boy and licked wherever he could. His tail drooped down. Then he took the corner of Johnny's coat in his mouth and tugged it again.

Johnny looked down into the soft brown eyes. Shadow was speaking to him as clearly as could be. "Come with me," his eyes were saying.

Johnny was puzzled. "Well, I'll come," he said at last. "But if it's just for nothing, I shall be cross with you."

Shadow took Johnny into the moonlit farmyard once more, and then took the path to the woods. Johnny

followed, more and more puzzled. But when at last he stood looking down at Dandy, he knew why Shadow had run from him, and why the dog had tugged at his coat!

"Oh Dandy! What's wrong?" cried Johnny, and he knelt down beside the tired dog. The moonlight glinted on the bright trap, and Johnny gave a cry of dismay.

"You've got your foot in a trap! Oh Dandy, you poor, poor thing! How long have you been here? Oh, how am I to open the trap?"

Dandy whined a little. He was so tired out with pain that he could hardly lift his head. Shadow pulled at the trap. Johnny looked at it carefully

99

saw how to open it. He must put his foot on one part, and then drag open the steel teeth.

The boy tried—and at last the cruel teeth parted, and there was Dandy's foot, free, but crushed and bleeding. The dog did not know at first that his foot was free, for it still hurt him terribly.

"Take your foot out before the trap shuts again!" cried Johnny. And Dandy painfully moved his poor foot. He stood up on three legs, holding his wounded foot high. It still hurt, though with a different pain now. But at any rate he was free. He could get away from that horrible steel thing that had held him prisoner!

The three of them went home slowly, for Dandy was tired.

Johnny woke his father and the two of them gently bathed and bound up the hurt foot.

"Dandy, if you *will* go off hunting by yourself like this, you *must* learn to look out for traps!" said the farmer. "Poor creature—you won't be much use looking after the sheep for a week or two. But your foot will mend. Go and sleep in the yard with Jessie, the farm-dog, to-night."

Dandy trotted off on three legs. He licked Shadow as he went.

"Thank you," he said. "You're a good friend. No wonder Johnny loves you best in the world!"

"But that's just what he doesn't do!" thought Shadow, sadly, as he lay down by the kitchen fire. "Johnny has said to-night that he doesn't want me in his bed. He is angry because I left him. But how I leave Dandy in pain?"

Johnny wondered where Shadow was. He was now in bed, waiting for the sheep-dog to come and jump up on his feet. But no Shadow came.

"Surely he doesn't think I'm still cross with him!" thought Johnny.

He went to the kitchen—and there was Shadow by the fire, ears and tail well down. "Shadow!" cried Johnny. "Come here! I want you on my bed. I think you're a good, clever dog to find poor Dandy like that, and fetch me to him. I understand why you left me now—and you were quite right. I'm sorry I was cross. Come here, Shadow!"

And Shadow came gladly, whining a little and licking the boy's bare legs. He lay down happily on Johnny's bed, nibbling the boy's toes with love. Nothing in the world mattered so long as Johnny wanted him close!

Spears for Impies

THE Impies were very small. They were funny little creatures, and they wandered about doing all kinds of little odd jobs for anyone they could.

They were honest, hard-working little things. Their chief was Nobbly-One, and he was called that because he had such bony knees.

They were trying to save up to buy a small caravan for themselves, so that they could go about in that instead of walking everywhere. Nobbly carried a bag of money and he never let it out of his sight.

Now one winter's day the Impies were journeying through the woods in search of work when they saw in the distance some small green creatures.

Nobbly stopped. "Look!" he whispered. "The green goblins! They know about our money. We must hide!" But the green goblins had seen them. It was of no use to hide. The goblins formed up in lines and the Impies saw that they had stout sticks with them.

"We've no weapons at all!" said Nobbly in despair. "Shall we run away?"

"They'll soon catch us!" said his little men. "No— let's climb this tree! Maybe we'll find a hole we can hide in."

So up they went. It was a beech tree, its branches quite bare. There was a hole some way up. The Impies swarmed inside. It was very warm and seemed to be full of soft fur!

"Gracious! There's a squirrel here asleep!" said Nobbly. But the squirrel soon woke up when he felt the little Impies scampering over him.

He uncurled his nose from his tail and looked at them.

"Hallo!" he said, pleased. "I know! You helped me to hide my nuts in the autumn. You showed me some very good places. I've forgotten them all now, but I know they were fine hidey-holes!"

"We've come here to hide from the green goblins," said Nobbly. "We've no weapons, you see. We can't fight them. If only we had some good sharp spears."

"The green goblins are climbing up the tree now!" cried a small Impy, peeping out of the hole.

"Look—can't you take some of the twigs of this beech tree for spears?" said the squirrel suddenly. "See how very very sharp the buds are—they will prick you and make you bleed if you run the points into you! They would make wonderful spears!"

"Oh, yes, yes!" cried the Impies, and they quickly broke off some of the twigs. They held them like spears, the sharp buds making the points.

And then what a shock for the green goblins!

The Impies met them with their sharp new spears and soon the goblins were racing down the branches of the beech tree trying to get away from the pricks and jabs!

They were soon caught! The squirrel helped the Impies and each goblin was taken back to the hole in the tree as a prisoner. But they were such dirty, smelly little things that the squirrel wouldn't have them with him!

"But what shall we do with them?" asked Nobbly. "We don't want to let them go now we've caught them. I'm going to march them off to the king!"

"*I* know what we'll do with them!" said the squirrel with a laugh. "You watch! I'll put them somewhere safe!"

And so he did! He took each little goblin and flung him hard into the next tree, which was a big horse-chestnut. And the goblins all stuck fast on to the big brown buds there and couldn't get away!

"There you are!" said the squirrel. "Caught as fast

as you please! They can stay there while you send word to the king to send his soldiers here to get them."

"But how is it they are stuck there?" cried Nobbly in surprise, watching the green goblins wriggling on the fat chestnut buds.

"Why, those buds are as sticky as glue!" said the squirrel. "Didn't you know?"

So they were. Nobbly was surprised. "You *are* clever!" he said to the squirrel. "You showed us how to use the sharp beech-buds for spears and now you have made the green goblins prisoners on the sticky chestnut buds. What a lot you know about trees!"

"Well—I live among them," said the squirrel. "Now goodbye—I'm off to sleep again. I *do* hope I remember where my nuts are when I wake up."

Two Good Turns

NEDDY was the little donkey belonging to Mr. Johns. Sam was the little boy who lived at the greengrocer's shop and helped his father to weigh the potatoes, and set out the cabbages and apples in neat rows.

Neddy passed by the shop each day. Sam was always ready for him with a bit of carrot or half an apple.

"You spoil that donkey of Mr. Johns," grumbled his father. "He's a lazy, stubborn little thing. Sometimes he stands still in the middle of the street and won't budge an inch."

"Mr. Johns isn't kind to him," said Sam. "He shouts at him and beats him. If I were a donkey *I'd* stand still in the middle of the road sometimes, if my master was unkind to me."

"Oh, you would, would you?" said his father. "Well, you'd get beaten even harder if *I* were your master. Donkeys like that don't deserve kind words and pats. Now, you go and get on with your work.

Fold up all those sacks and stack them neatly in the corner."

Neddy came up the hill by the shop the next day, and Sam flew out to give him an apple.

But Mr. Johns wouldn't let the donkey stop for it.

"He's been stubborn again!" he shouted angrily. "Backed into a gate and broke a bit off the back of the cart. He's not to have any treats. Come up, there! You bad fellow!"

Sam was sad. Neddy was sad too, because he did like an apple—and, more than that, he liked the loving words Sam spoke to him and the feel of Sam's hands on his neck. Ah, if only he had a master like that boy! He'd never be stubborn again.

The winter came. The weather grew colder and colder. Snow came, and it froze. More snow came, and

that froze too, till the roads were like slippery ice. Cars could no longer go up the hill by Sam's shop.

But the little grey donkey still came, sliding and slipping, pulling the heavy cart up the hill.

"It's a shame," thought Sam, watching. "Poor little thing—it's terribly hard not to slip just here, where the hill is so steep. Neddy will break his legs one day!"

The next day the donkey stopped outside the shop. Mr. Johns lashed him with the whip. "Go on with you! What's the matter? You're the laziest animal there ever was."

Neddy started off again, but his feet slipped all the time. Sam watched him, terrified that he would fall and break a leg. Mr. Johns whipped him again.

Sam darted into the shop. He went to where the pile of sacks was, in a corner. He rushed out with them. He went to the donkey and flung a sack under his feet. Then he put another in front of him, and a

third one higher up. He made a whole pathway of sacks—and the little donkey found firm footing on them and pulled the cart safely up the steepest bit. He looked round gratefully at Sam. Nice boy, kind boy! his big donkey-eyes said.

"He could have got up without all that," shouted Mr. Johns grumpily. "Always making a fuss of Neddy! I tell you he's just a lazy, stupid beast, and I'd be glad to get rid of him!"

Next day the frost was harder than ever. Sam was waiting with the sacks, and he made the same path for Neddy as the day before. The little donkey didn't slip at all. He was very pleased.

It was Wednesday and a half-holiday for Sam. What should he do? "I think I'll go down to the pond, Dad," he said. "Not the one all the boys go to, because that's so crowded and I do want a good slide. I'll go to Bolter's Pond—that won't be crowded at all."

He went to Bolter's Pond, and there were only two boys on it, trying it. "It's quite hard!" they yelled to Sam. "Come and try."

The boys soon left, and Sam thought he would make a really good long slide. Soon he had a real beauty, and enjoyed himself immensely.

And then—and then there suddenly came a loud CRACK! And the ice split right across as Sam was sliding. He couldn't stop himself and slid straight into the crack, where the water was showing black below. In he went and gasped with the icy cold. He caught hold of the freezing edges of the ice and shouted loudly: "Help! Help! Save me!"

"If only somebody would give a party!" he said to himself. "A real, good, old-fashioned party, with heaps of jellies and trifles and blancmanges and sandwiches and chocolate biscuits and lemonade! If only somebody would!"

One day Hoppitty mentioned his idea of a party to Brock the badger.

Brock was a kind and generous animal, and he really loved being friendly to everyone. He listened to everything that Hoppitty said, and nodded his striped head gravely.

"Why don't *you* give a party, Hoppitty, as you are so anxious to have one?" asked Brock.

"Well, you see, I'm very poor," exclaimed Hoppitty. "I'd *love* to give one, but it wouldn't be much of a party, I'm afraid, Brock—just a few grass sandwiches, that's all! Now if *you* gave a party—my word, how grand that would be! How people would love to come!"

"It *might* be a good idea," said the badger, who loved having all his friends around him. "Yes—I'll give one, Hoppitty. You shall make out the list of guests and write the invitations, for I'm no good at that sort of thing. I'll see to the food—you see to the other part."

Hoppitty was delighted—especially as a very clever idea had come into his long-eared head!

"Now just suppose I ask all those animals who go to sleep for the winter!" he said to himself. "They won't be able to come to the party, of course—so when I arrive I'll be the only guest, for *I* don't sleep in the cold weather. And I can eat everything! My word, that *is* a good idea!"

He did a little jig of joy as he thought of it. Then he sat down to think again. "Whom shall I ask?" he said. "Well now, Prickles the hedgehog sleeps in the winter-time, so I'll ask him. And Dozy the dormouse does too—and so does Flitter the bat. That's three. Then there's Bushy the red squirrel. He's nearly always asleep in the winter-time. And Slither the snake too. I found him asleep in the hollow tree last winter, so I know he doesn't like the cold weather. Oh, and Croak the frog and Crawler the toad, of course! They sleep soundly in the winter-time!"

Very soon Hoppitty had sent out the invitations for the seven guests. He told Brock about them—but he

didn't tell the badger that each of the guests would be fast asleep by the time the party-day came! Oh no—Hoppitty was really being very clever.

"Well, they sound all right," said Brock, pleased. "With ourselves, that makes nine. A very nice number for a party. And here is the list of things we're going to eat, Hoppitty."

He handed Hoppitty a list. The rabbit's eyes nearly fell out of his head as he read it.

"Twenty radish sandwiches. Twenty lettuce sandwiches. Twenty tomato rolls. Six chocolate blancmanges. Six trifles. Six pink jellies. Six yellow jellies. Two pounds of chocolate biscuits. Six jugs of sweet lemonade."

"Oh, fine, fine!" said Hoppitty. "This will be the best party ever given in Bluebell Wood, Brock. You are really most generous. Now, what about the date? I think the first of November would be a good time."

"Very well," said Brock, who hadn't much idea of time. "I've got a calendar on the wall of my den. I tear a day off each morning. I shall know when November the first is coming near. You can depend on me."

All the guests answered their invitations, and they all said they would come. Hoppitty grinned when he read the letters.

"They will all be fast asleep for the winter!" he chuckled. "None of them will be able to come then— and I shall have the finest feast I've ever had. Brock will eat a few of the things, I dare say—but I'll eat the most."

Hoppitty could hardly wait till November the
first. Frosts came in October, and the animals shivered.
The last swallows left. The leaves fell, and a good
many of the smaller animals began to feel very sleepy.

The hedgehog found a hole in a bank, lined it
with moss and dead leaves, and fell fast asleep. The
dormouse slept in a cosy hole underneath a tree-root.
The snake found a hollow tree and coiled up there
with its brothers. The toad slept soundly under a
big mossy stone, and the frog went down to the mud
at the bottom of the pond. The squirrel decided to
take a nap too, till a warm spell came, and the bat
shivered and went to hang himself upside down in an
old barn he knew.

November the first came at last—a fine cold day with a round red sun in the sky. Hoppitty was tremendously excited. His sister had knitted him a new blue scarf to wear for the party, so he really looked very grand.

"I'll try and bring you home a lettuce sandwich," he promised her. "Now, it's four o'clock—I must be off. My, there *will* be a spread in Brock's den!"

He sped off, chuckling to think that all the other guests were fast asleep. How silly they were—and how clever *he* was!

He came to Brock's hole. It was blocked up, but there was a bell-pull outside. Hoppitty rang it and heard the bell jangling loudly. Nobody came to open the hole.

Hoppitty rang again. Still there was no answer. The rabbit was puzzled and cross. This was November the first—and Brock should have got everything ready! Wherever was he?

"Brock!" shouted Hoppitty. "Do come and open the door! It's me! Hurry, because it's cold standing out here."

There was no anwer at all. Hoppitty began to pull at the bracken that was stuffing up the hole, but it was so firmly wedged in that he couldn't move it.

"I say, Brock!" he called, drumming on the ground with his hind feet. "Come at once!"

A thin red nose poked out of a hole nearby, and Rufus the fox looked at Hoppitty with a sly grin.

"Why do you want Brock?" he asked.

"Because he's giving a party to-day," said Hoppitty, rather scared of the fox. "I can't *think* why he doesn't come to the door!"

"But *I* can," said Rufus slyly. "He's asleep."

"Asleep!" cried Hoppitty. "You don't really mean that?"

"Of course I do," said the fox. "Don't you know that badgers sleep in the winter-time, the same as hedgehogs and dormice and snakes? Brock stuffed up his hole two weeks ago, and he and his family are snoring away deep down at the bottom. I know, because I've heard them. There won't be any party to-day."

"Oh dear!" wailed Hoppitty in despair. "And I did so want a really good tea. I'm terribly hungry."

"So am I!" said Rufus the fox, coming out of his

hole. "I want a really good tea too—a rabbit tea!"

He shot after the frightened bunny, who ran for his life. He was very nearly caught, for the ends of his new blue scarf flew out behind him and the fox caught one of them in his teeth. But the scarf tore in half, and Hoppitty just managed to run down his burrow in time, startling his sister almost out of her skin when he rushed full-tilt into her.

He told her all about the party, and how he had had such a good idea, asking guests that he knew couldn't come.

"But I didn't think that Brock the badger would be asleep too," he said sadly.

"The trouble with you is that you're much too greedy and think yourself too clever," said his sister, who was cross about his torn scarf. "I'm glad this has happened. Perhaps it will teach you a lesson."

"It will," said Hoppitty mournfully. "I'll never do such a thing again!"

Peter's Good Turn

PETER was a Boy Scout. Every day he had to do a good turn to somebody, and he never, never forgot, whatever happened.

Sometimes he ran an errand for his mother. That was one good turn. Sometimes he fetched the paper for his father. That was another good turn.

Sometimes he picked up a child who had fallen down, and he wound his own hanky round the hurt knee. That was another good turn.

"So long as I can find a good turn each day, I've kept my promise," thought Peter. "But I shall be sad if I can't find a good turn—I would have to break my promise."

Well, there came a day when Peter simply couldn't seem to find a good turn to do. His mother didn't want any errands running. In fact, she told Peter not to come bothering her, for she was busy.

His father was out at work. Mrs. Brown next door said she didn't want anything at all. No child fell down in the streets. No bird fell out of a nest. Nobody wanted any letters posted. It was very tiresome.

"How can I possibly do a good turn if there isn't one to be done?" wondered Peter. "Well, perhaps I'd better go and look round a bit. I may find one to do."

So off he went for a walk. It was after tea, so there wasn't much time till bedtime, but Peter meant to find a good turn to do *some*how!

When he came into Pond Lane, he saw a puppy dog. It was standing in the gutter. Peter knew the puppy. It was Gip, who belonged to Mr. George. He whistled.

"Phee! Pheee! Phee!"

Gip whined, but he didn't come. "Gip, Gip! Come along!" shouted Peter. "I'm out for a walk!"

Still Gip didn't move, but only yelped pitifully. "There must be something wrong!" thought Peter, and he ran to see.

What *do* you think had happened? Poor Gip had got his paw caught in the grating of the drain! He had put it there to try to catch the water that he saw winking at him below the drain—and now he couldn't get his paw out again! He had twisted it round so that it was stuck more tightly than ever!

"You poor fellow!" said Peter, and he knelt down beside him. "You know, Gip, I've been looking and looking for a good turn to do to-day—and you're my good turn! You see, Gip, I have to do a good turn every day. I've promised to, and I must never break a promise. I'm a Boy Scout. I expect you've seen me in my uniform."

All the time he was talking, Peter was trying to get Gip's paw out of the drain. He tried it this way and he tried it that way. The puppy whined. He licked Peter's ear and listened to all he said.

Peter twisted the little fat paw round to the right—and it suddenly slipped out of the grating! It was swollen and painful, and the puppy limped, holding his foot up as he went.

"My good turn to you isn't finished yet," said Peter. "Come along to the stream and let me bathe your paw. Then the swelling will go down."

So the boy bathed the swollen paw in the cool water. The puppy was glad to feel the pain going. He licked Peter again. He thought it was a very good idea to do a good turn to somebody every day. He thought in his puppy mind that he would do the same! He would be a Boy Scout too!

He ran home on all four paws. Peter went home too, very happy because he had found his good turn to do.

And the very next day Gip paid Peter back for his good turn. It was really very strange, but it just happened all of a sudden.

Gip was out, looking for *his* good turn to do. Suddenly he smelt the smell of Peter, and he looked

for him. He saw Peter crossing the road—and he saw, too, a big car coming at a tremendous speed. It would certainly knock Peter down! There was no time for anybody to pull the boy back.

But what was this? A brown furry body suddenly hurled itself into the road, and flung itself on Peter's back. The boy went flying across the road and fell flat on his face with the shock.

The car missed him by about two inches. Gip had saved Peter's life! Everyone ran up and began to pat the dog, and pick Peter up, and talk about the wonderful thing the dog had done.

"Oh, Gip, it's *you* that saved my life, is it!" cried Peter, and he hugged the puppy. "You were my good turn yesterday, and I was yours to-day! You're a good little Scout dog. You really are!"

128

Gip wagged his tail so hard that it looked like a windmill in the wind!

Then up came a newspaper man, who wanted to write all about the clever puppy in his newspaper, and when he heard what Peter said, what *do* you think he did? Why, he went to buy a Scout hat and a Scout pole for Gip, and he took a picture of Peter and Gip together—Peter in his Scout uniform, and Gip in his Scout hat, holding the pole!

They send a message to you, and it's this: "Do a good turn every day, if you can!"

Very well—we will!

The Sneezing Dog

THERE was once a dog called Collie, and, as you can guess, he was a collie-dog. He lived in a yard, and he had a big kennel to himself, because he was a big dog. He was on a chain, because he had to guard his master's house, and Mr. Snoot didn't want him wandering about loose, far away from the house.

So Collie was always tied up, except when Mr. Snoot took him out for a walk. He was often very bored. It wasn't much fun to sit night and day inside or outside his kennel, when he wanted to go and hunt rabbits or see his friends. All he could do was to bark loudly when any stranger came to the yard.

That was what Mr. Snoot wanted him to do. Mr. Snoot was a miser, and he had a good deal of money hidden up the chimney-place in his kitchen. As soon as he heard Collie bark he was warned of people coming, and he could look out for them.

When the winter came Mr. Snoot put more blankets on his bed. He bought extra milk from the milkman so that he could warm it up at night and put it beside his bed in a flask to keep it hot. He had a tin of his favourite biscuits there too to eat with the hot milk. He didn't mind waking up at night then, for he would pour himself out a glass of hot milk and eat a few biscuits. Then he would pop down into his kitchen, put his hand up the chimney, feel to see if his money-bag was there, and go back to bed again, quite happy.

He would pull his lovely warm blankets over his head, and go peacefully to sleep, knowing that if any tramp or robber came along, Collie would bark loudly to tell him.

The days were cold. The nights were colder. Collie had some straw in his kennel to lie on, but not much, and what there was was rather flattened down by the weight of his big body. He shivered. It made his chain rattle when he shivered. He got further into his kennel and tried to spread the straw round himself, but there wasn't enough.

He went out to his bowl to get a drink, and to see if there were any biscuits left. Perhaps a meal would warm him up a bit. But alas, the water had frozen hard. His dinner-bowl was quite empty.

Poor Collie! He went back into his kennel, and wished that Mr. Snoot had swung it round to face the other way, because the cold north wind came blowing straight into the kennel. How could a dog possibly get warm with a wind like that blowing at him all the time!

Collie felt colder and colder. He shivered more and more. Then he felt a sneeze coming. It was a big one. "A-a-a-a-a-WHOOOOOSH-ooooo!" sneezed Collie loudly.

There was a squeal from outside, a squeal of fright. Then a little voice said, "What did you do that for? You blew me off my feet!"

Collie stuck his nose outside in surprise. Who was this? He hadn't heard anyone. Ought he to bark?

Outside stood a small man, dressed in a brown tunic, and brown stockings and shoes. He wore a pointed hat, and had a long grey beard. His bright blue eyes twinkled like stars in a frosty night.

"Hallo!" said Collie surprised. "One of the little folk, I suppose? What are you doing here at this time of night?"

"I got called out to a robin who's half-frozen," said the brownie. "I'm a doctor, you know. Dr. Help-a-Bit. You may have heard of me."

"Well, I haven't really," said Collie. "Did I almost blow you off your feet just now when I sneezed?"

"Right off," said Dr. Help-a-Bit. "I got an awful shock. What's the matter with you, sneezing like that? And why do you keep rattling your chain?"

"Well, brownie, I don't mean to rattle it, but I can't help it, because I'm so cold," said Collie. "It's my shivering that rattles the chain."

"What a shame!" said the brownie. "Get out of your kennel, and go and bark at the house door. They'll have to let you into the warmth then."

"I can't," said Collie. "I'm chained. Can't you see? I'm terribly cold because I can't run about to keep myself warm, and I haven't enough straw to cuddle down in."

"I can't have this sort of thing," said Dr. Help-a-Bit, looking very fierce all of a sudden. "I'll go and see your master about it. Poor creature! How can anyone treat you like that? I'll go and wake your master."

Before Collie could stop him the brownie had gone to the back door, opened it with a key he had, and gone inside. He went upstairs, drawn there by a loud noise of snoring. He came to Mr. Snoot's bedroom. By the light of the little lamp that Mr. Snoot always left burning, the brownie saw the fat old man lying fast asleep in bed.

"Wake up!" said the brownie sternly. Mr. Snoot didn't stir. The brownie gave him a prod. Still Mr. Snoot didn't wake. Then Dr. Help-a-Bit's eyes gleamed.

He had noticed the great pile of warm, woolly blankets that Mr. Snoot had on his bed. He saw the flask of hot milk by the bedside and the tin of biscuits.

How pleased a cold and hungry dog would be with all those things.

The brownie put the tin of biscuits in one pocket and the flask of hot milk into another. Then, softly pulling at the pile of woolly blankets, he dragged them all off the bed, tucked them round his shoulders to carry, and went downstairs again. Mr. Snoot had nothing on him except for a thin sheet. All his blankets had gone.

Dr. Help-a-Bit took everything outside. "Here you are," he said to Collie, pouring the milk into the bowl. "Drink it up while it's hot. And eat these biscuits— you'll like them. Then I'll pack your kennel with these fine blankets and you'll be as warm as toast, as soon as you cuddle down in them."

Collie was overjoyed. He lapped up the hot milk. He crunched up the delicious biscuits. Then he squeezed into the fleecy blankets and the brownie pulled them closely round him. "I'm sorry I'm not strong enough to swing your kennel away from the cold north wind," he said. "But I don't somehow think you'll feel the cold now!"

Collie didn't! He slept all night long in warmth and comfort, a very happy dog. How kind of the brownie to bother about him like that! Collie wished he could do something in return, but he couldn't think of anything.

Now about half an hour later, Mr. Snoot awoke shivering with cold. He put out his hand and felt for his blankets. They weren't there. They must have fallen on the floor, he thought. He sat up and looked.

What a very extraordinary thing—they weren't on the floor either. In fact, they were nowhere to be seen.

Cold, puzzled and frightened, Mr. Snoot took up his flask to pour out a glass of hot milk. It was empty! The brownie had carefully taken it back with the biscuit tin and put them in their place beside Mr. Snoot's bed. No biscuits—no milk—no blankets! Mr. Snoot was alarmed. He thought there must surely be burglars about—and yet Collie hadn't barked!

He crept downstairs and felt for his money-bag up

the chimney. It was still there. He pulled it down, and dragged it upstairs. He locked the door and looked round for a bed-covering. There was nothing he could use except for a table-cloth, and that wasn't very warm! So Mr. Snoot shivered all night long, and couldn't sleep at all.

In the morning he went to scold Collie for letting a thief come in the night without barking at him. He saw something in Collie's kennel, and *how* astonished he was to find that all his blankets were stuffed there! He pulled them out in amazement.

"Who did this?" he said sternly to Collie. "It couldn't have been you because you are always chained up. It's a very silly joke, whoever did it. I am not pleased."

Well, as he had taken the blankets away, poor Collie was as cold as ever the next night. But along came the brownie again to see if he was all right—and how angry he was when he found that Mr. Snoot had taken away the blankets, but hadn't bothered to give poor Collie any more straw—or even to give him water instead of the ice in his bowl.

"Well, Snoot can shiver all night again," he said, grimly. "I'm going to get his blankets, his hot milk and his biscuits once more!"

So into the house he went, up the stairs and into the bedroom. Once again he pulled the blankets off the snoring Mr. Snoot, and took his flask of hot milk and his biscuits. And once again Collie lapped eagerly, crunched the biscuits and then snuggled down in the blankets.

And once more poor Mr. Snoot awoke shivering with the cold, and looked for the blankets that were not there! He was really very frightened when he found that they had disappeared again!

He lighted a lantern, put on his dressing-gown, and went downstairs and out into the yard. Yes, just as he had thought, Collie had his blankets again; and what was this in his bowl—a drop of milk—and a few crumbs of his best biscuits! So that was where his things were going! Mr. Snoot was angry.

He tried to pull the blankets out of Collie's kennel. But Collie held on to them, and it looked as if they would be torn to pieces!

"I *must* have my blankets!" roared Mr. Snoot. "I shall freeze at night if I don't."

"And what about your dog, you selfish fellow?" said a stern voice nearby. Mr. Snoot turned and saw the brownie looking at him. "Hardly any straw in his bitterly cold kennel, no water to drink—shivering all night long, poor thing. You ought to be ashamed of yourself. Collie, let go of the blankets. I've an idea!"

Collie let go. Mr. Snoot bent to snatch them, but the brownie took them first. He glared at Mr. Snoot. "You'll stay out here in this yard all night long, and see what it is like! I'm going to take Collie upstairs and put him into your bed and cover him with these blankets. You stay here and pretend to be him. See how you like it!"

Mr. Snoot watched the brownie and Collie going indoors. Dr. Help-a-Bit had undone the chain, so Collie was free. Mr. Snoot tried to go after them, but the brownie had put magic into his slippers and he couldn't move a step out of the cold, windy yard.

Weeping with the cold, Mr. Snoot crept into the kennel to try to get a bit warmer. But the north wind blew in strongly. There was too little straw to nestle in. He shivered so much that the kennel creaked all night long.

But Collie slept well, tucked in Mr. Snoot's comfortable bed. What a night he had! Mr. Snoot found him there in the morning when he went upstairs. The magic went from his slippers at dawn, and he was able to go into the house. Collie awoke and looked at him, expecting him to be very angry.

But Mr. Snoot wasn't. He was strangely humble. He spoke to Collie. "I didn't know how cold it was out there without enough straw. I didn't know how the wind blew into your kennel. I didn't see that your water was frozen. I beg your pardon. Forgive me. I have had a most dreadful night, the kind of night you must often have had. Poor Collie!"

Collie licked Mr. Snoot's hand. And that day Mr. Snoot filled the kennel with warm straw and swung it right away from the wind. He put fresh water down and a big dish of biscuits and bones. He didn't put Collie on the chain again.

Collie spoke to the brownie gratefully when he next saw him. "Thank you!" he said. "I'm very happy now—and all because I did that very big sneeze one night and blew you off your feet!"

The Girl With Whiskers

THERE was once a girl called Betty who teased animals. She had a dog, and two cats, and three rabbits down the garden, and she teased them all. She pulled the cats' tails, she pulled the dog's whiskers, and she swung the rabbits round by their ears.

The rabbits and the cats ran whenever they saw her. The rabbits hid at the back of the cage, and the cats jumped over the wall. Only the dog stayed where he was, for, surprising as it may seem, he loved Betty.

"However can you love her?" said one of the cats. "Hateful girl! You don't *really* love her, do you, Bonzo?"

"It's funny, but I do," said Bonzo. "That's the way dogs are made, you know. They can't help loving the family they live with! I don't like my whiskers being pulled, and I hate having things tied to my tail, as Betty does sometimes—but I'd do anything for her, really I would!"

"Then we think you're just silly!" said the cats, and they walked off with their tails in the air.

One day Betty went for a walk, and she passed a funny little house she had never seen before. Lying asleep on the front path was a puppy. He had the longest whiskers that Betty had ever seen in her life! She stared at them in surprise.

She crept up to the puppy, bent down and took hold of his whiskers. The naughty little tease pulled the whiskers hard. The puppy woke up with a squeal. Betty pulled his fine whiskers again, and he yelped and tried to get away.

Betty laughed—and just as she let go of the puppy's whiskers, the door of the queer little house flew open and an old woman looked out.

"Don't you steal my puppy's fine whiskers!" she cried. "I've got some, just like them, that you can have for yourself."

She ran down the path with a box in her hand. In it were some long green whiskers. In a trice the old woman dabbed them hard on to Betty's pink cheeks. They stuck there, sticking out at each side, looking very peculiar!

Betty gave a scream. "I wasn't stealing his whiskers!" she cried. "I was teasing him! Take these horrid green whiskers away!"

"*Tea*sing him!" cried the old woman in anger. "You horrid girl! *Keep* the whiskers! It will serve you right to have something you don't want!"

She slammed the door. Betty ran home crying, holding her hands in front of her face so that no

one would see her awful green whiskers.

She slipped in at the garden door and went up to her room. She looked at herself in the glass—oh dear, oh dear, what a peculiar sight she was! Green whiskers, as long as a cat's or a dog's, grew out from her cheeks, just by her mouth! Betty pulled at them, trying to get them off.

They wouldn't come off at all! They were really growing! Betty sobbed in fright and pain. She looked dreadful with green whiskers.

"It hurts me to pull them, it hurts me!" she wept. "Oh, how I must have hurt that little puppy! Oh, whatever shall I do?"

There was a pattering of feet in the room, and Bonzo the dog came in. He had heard Betty crying and had come to see what the matter was. Although she had pulled his ears hard that morning and made him yelp, he couldn't bear to hear her crying.

He pushed his nose on to her knee, and tried to love Betty. She looked at him—and he saw her astonishing green whiskers. He was very surprised.

"Oh, Bonzo, I pulled a puppy's whiskers this morning, and a horrid old woman came out and stuck some on my cheeks," sobbed Betty. "And now they're growing there, and I can't pull them off. I daren't go to school. I daren't go out at all, because people will laugh at me so much. Oh, I'm so unhappy! Whatever shall I do?"

Bonzo licked Betty's hand. He was very surprised. He knew quite well who the old woman was, and he had seen the puppy with the enormous whiskers. To think that poor Betty should have to wear whiskers too! She sobbed, and the dog felt more and more unhappy.

He forgot that Betty had teased him. He forgot that she had been unkind very often and that the cats and rabbits hated her. He only remembered that here was a little girl in trouble, and he wanted to help her. He was as loving and as faithful as all dogs are.

He pulled Betty's dress gently. She looked down at him. He pulled her again. He wanted her to go with him. She got up and followed Bonzo.

He pulled her downstairs and out into the garden. He took her down the lane till she came to the cottage where the old woman lived. He left her outside and went into the house himself, stopping to sniff at the long-whiskered puppy as he went.

The old woman was there. The dog began to talk to her, for the old woman was partly a fairy and could understand what he said.

"Mistress, take the whiskers away from Betty!" begged Bonzo. "She is so unhappy. Please, do take them away."

"She is an unkind little girl and deserves a punishment," said the old woman.

"Well, she has been punished enough now," said Bonzo. "You've no idea how she cried and cried! I love her and it makes me unhappy."

"You *love* her!" cried the old woman. "Well, dear me, if you love her there must be some good in her.

For your sake and because of your loving heart, I will take the whiskers away, Bonzo. But I'll give her twice as many if she teases any animal again."

The old woman ran down the path to Betty, who was crying outside the gate. She put out her hand and snatched off Betty's green whiskers. The little girl gave a scream, for it hurt her very much.

"Scream away!" said the old woman. "You've made many an animal squeal and yelp, *I* know. There! Your whiskers are out! I've taken them away because your loving dog has begged me to. He says he loves you and doesn't want you to be unhappy. Your dog is a better creature than you are, Betty!"

Betty knelt down and put her arms round Bonzo, who licked her face in joy. "Thank you for helping me, Bonzo," she said. "Thank you for loving me enough, though I've been so horrid. Now I'll show you how nice I can be! I promise you I will!"

Do you think she'll keep her word? Well, if she doesn't, she'll have to wear green whiskers again—I'm certain of that!

The Angry Puppy

THERE was once a puppy who stole a string of sausages from the kitchen. He was whipped very hard for his naughtiness, and he was angry.

"I won't stay here and be treated like this!" he yelped. "Horrid people! I'll run away and go to live with animals. I shall be happier then."

So he ran off. Soon he came to a great brown horse, feeding in a field. He spoke to him.

"May I come and live with you?" he asked.

"Certainly!" said the horse. "You will have grass to eat. You will have a heavy saddle to carry. And you will learn to paw the ground, like this!"

He pawed the ground so hard that a clod of earth flew up and struck the surprised puppy on the nose.

"I don't like you," he said to the horse, very angrily. "I should hate to eat grass. I won't carry a heavy saddle. And I think that pawing the ground as you do is silly!"

He trotted off again, and came to where a big cat
was stretched out on the ground, sunning herself. The
puppy spoke to her.

"May I come and live with you?" he asked.

"Certainly!" said the cat. "You will learn to catch
birds to eat. You will have to keep down the mice.
And you must learn to scratch, like this!"

The cat put out her claws and scratched the puppy
on the leg. He was very angry.

"I don't like you," he said to the cat. "I should hate
to catch birds. I wouldn't bother myself to catch
mice. And I think it would be silly to learn to scratch!"

He ran off, and the cat laughed to herself. Soon he
came to a big white goose, and he ran up to her.

"May I come and live with you?" he asked.

"Certainly!" said the goose with a cackle. "You
will have to waddle like me. You will have to cackle
like this—cackle, cackle, cackle! And you will learn
to peck, like this!"

The goose put out her great beak and pecked the puppy's tail. She almost pecked it off! The puppy yelped, and was very cross.

"I don't like you," he said. "I should hate to waddle as clumsily as you. I wouldn't like to cackle at all—and I think pecking is silly!"

He ran off, yelping angrily. He was a very cross little pup indeed. Soon he came to where a red fox was ambling along, and he spoke to him.

"May I come and live with you?"

"Certainly!" said the fox, and he grinned at the small puppy. "You will have to learn to bark just like me—oof, oof, oof! You will be chased by dogs. And you must learn to snap, like this!"

He snapped at the puppy and almost bit the end of his nose off. The puppy jumped back in alarm.

"I don't like you," he said. "I should hate to bark like a fox instead of a dog. I should hate to be hunted by a pack of dogs—and to snap suddenly like that isn't at all nice!"

He ran off, and came to where a company of ducks was lying at ease by the water-side. The puppy spoke to them.

"May I come and live with you?" he asked.

"Certainly!" said the ducks. "You must quack like this—quack-quack-quack! You must burrow in the mud of the pond. And you must swim, like this!"

They all jumped into the pond and splashed the puppy from head to foot. He was very angry. He shook himself and yelped at the ducks:

"I don't like you! I think quacking is silly, and as

for burrowing in the mud, it's a horrible thing to do. And if swimming means getting wet all over, it's a thing I'll never learn!"

He ran off, wet and miserable. He was tired and hungry and lonely. He ran and ran, and at last found himself at his own back door. His mistress was there and she went to welcome him.

"You poor little puppy! I thought you must be lost! Come along in and get dry and warm. I'll give you some hot milk to drink, a sweet biscuit, and a bone. You shall lie down in your own cosy basket and be happy!"

"Good gracious!" said the puppy to himself, as he lay in his warm basket chewing a delicious bone, with his mistress patting him lovingly. "Good gracious! What did I want to run away for? Why did I want to live with anyone else? I'll stay at home in future and BE GOOD!"

Well, he did stay at home, and he grew into a fine big dog. But he isn't always good, though his mistress loves him, good or naughty. I know, because he lives next door to me!